"This Is Dangerous."

"You think so?" Cameron asked sarcastically.

"I know so," Janine confirmed.

"But it's fun," he offered, hoping for another kiss.

"Yes, I'll certainly admit that."

"And I think we're both enjoying it."

She loved this light side of him, a side she hadn't seen before this evening. She wondered how often he allowed himself to unbend and tease in this way. "Cameron, neither of us is the type to lose our heads and hearts in passion."

"We're not?"

"Uh-uh."

"You're sure?"

"Uh-uh."

"So what do you suggest we do?"

"Go to bed."

"Hell of an idea! Let's!"

Dear Reader,

Welcome to Silhouette Desire! The fabulous things we have to offer you in Silhouette Desire just keep on coming. October is simply chock-full of delicious goodies to keep even the most picky romance reader happy all month long.

First, we have a thrilling new *Man of the Month* book from talented author Paula Detmer Riggs. It's called *A Man of Honor,* and I know Max Kaler is a hero you'll never forget.

Next, Annette Broadrick's SONS OF TEXAS series continues with *Courtship Texas Style!* Please *don't* worry if you didn't catch the beginning of this series, because each of the SONS OF TEXAS stands alone (and how!).

For those of you who are Lass Small fans—and you all know who you are!—her connecting series about those FABULOUS BROWN BROTHERS continues with *Two Halves.* Again, please don't fret if you haven't read about the *other* Brown Brothers, because Mike Brown is a hero in his own right!

I'm always thrilled to be able to introduce new authors to the Silhouette Desire family, and Anne Marie Winston is someone you'll be seeing a lot of in the future. Her first published book ever, *Best Kept Secrets,* is highlighted this month as a PREMIERE title. Watch for future Desire books by this talented newcomer in Spring 1993.

This month is completed in a most delightful way with Jackie Merritt's *Black Creek Ranch* (a new book by Jackie is always a thrill) and Donna Carlisle's *It's Only Make Believe.*

As for November... well, I'd tell you all about it, but I've run out of space. You'll just have to wait!

So until next month, happy reading,

Lucia Macro
Senior Editor

ANNETTE BROADRICK

COURTSHIP TEXAS STYLE!

SILHOUETTE *Desire*
Published by Silhouette Books New York
America's Publisher of Contemporary Romance

SILHOUETTE BOOKS
300 East 42nd St., New York, N.Y. 10017

COURTSHIP TEXAS STYLE!

ISBN: 0-373-05739-3

First Silhouette Books printing October 1992

ANNETTE BROADRICK

lives on the shores of Lake of the Ozarks in Missouri, where she spends her time doing what she loves most—reading and writing romance fiction. Since 1984, when her first book was published, Annette has been delighting her readers with her imaginative and innovative style. In addition to being nominated by *Romantic Times* magazine as one of the Best New Authors of that year, she has also won the *Romantic Times* Reviewer's Choice Award for Best in its Series for *Heat of the Night, Mystery Lover* and *Irresistible,* the *Romantic Times* WISH Award for her hero in *Strange Enchantment* and the *Romantic Times* Lifetime Achievement Award for Series Romance.

One

Without warning, bright lights leaped in front of the car, blinding him. Cameron swerved in a desperate attempt to miss the idiot who had suddenly appeared in the roadway ahead. His wife's scream echoed around him as the lights loomed ever larger, filling the windshield of the car with brilliance. He broke out in a cold sweat, his clammy hands clutching the steering wheel. He could feel his chest pounding, his body shaking. The metallic taste of fear filled his mouth.

He fought for control in a herculean effort to avoid a collision, feverishly regretting that he'd driven the small foreign sports car rather than their sedan.

Despite everything he could do, the larger car slammed into them and he knew with a sickening certainty that he had lost what little control he had.

They began to spin, faster and faster, rolling over and over until—

"Aaaugh!"

Cameron jerked into a sitting position and groaned, burying his head in his hands. He was drenched with sweat and was shaking. His heart pounded in his chest like an overworked piston. He ran a trembling hand through his hair, shoving it off his forehead, forcing himself awake.

My God! Was he never going to stop dreaming about the wreck? Almost four years had passed since the night of the accident that had killed his wife, yet it continued to haunt him.

He shoved the twisted sheets away from his legs and stumbled out of bed. He felt for his cigarettes and lighter on the bedside table without turning on a lamp, knowing they were never more than a hand's reach away. After lighting one, he made his way over to the window and stared out at the turbulence of a south Texas spring storm.

Perhaps the bright flashes of lightning followed by crashing thunder had triggered his recurring dream. He hadn't dreamed about the horror of that night in several months, and he'd begun to believe the nightmares were buried at long last.

Obviously he had been wrong.

He took a long drag from the cigarette, feeling the smoke curl its way into his lungs, knowing he was slowly killing himself with his habit and not giving a damn.

Hard-driving rain slashed the window glass. He shook his head in resignation. Much more of this spring rain and the whole ranch would be washed away.

During the midnight drive from San Antonio, he had listened to agitated announcers on the radio warn of flooding in low areas. For the past week the papers had been full of reports about flash flooding, damaging winds and destructive rainfall. He had witnessed the results firsthand when he turned off the highway and followed the six miles of private road to the main buildings of his family's ranch. Both bridges along the road were flooded with racing water. He had barely managed to inch his way across the last one.

Because he hadn't left his office until after midnight, he had considered sleeping at his condo in San Antonio, but he had felt too wired to sleep and had headed south toward the ranch, instead. The hour-and-a-half drive sometimes soothed him, gave him a chance to unwind. He hadn't counted on the weather continuing to be so wild.

He hadn't visited the ranch in almost three weeks. The guilt that constantly lived with him stirred at the thought. Three weeks had passed since he'd seen his daughter, Trisha. Three weeks without seeing her father was asking a great deal of a motherless five-year-old child.

He stubbed out the cigarette, then scrubbed his hand across his face. He reminded himself that Trisha was far from being neglected. Between his aunt Letty doting on her and the constant entertainment provided by Angie and Rosie, two of the family's employees, his daughter was far from being a waif. Still, he knew they weren't enough. His daily telephone conversations with Trisha made him very much aware of her feelings on the subject. She was always asking when he was going to come see her. He had promised that, no matter what, he would be there this weekend.

He was a man who never broke his promises. No matter how tired he was, nor how much work had stacked up at the office, he would be there.

He loved Trisha dearly. How could he not? She was his last link to Andrea, the woman he had loved so much. Trisha looked so much like Andrea that he was forever reminded of her.

He and Andrea had been on their way to the ranch to pick up Trisha that fateful night four years ago. Andrea had been so happy. They had spent the evening with some of his business associates. Letty had suggested they leave the baby for the whole weekend, but Andrea thought the teething infant would be too fretful without her mother there to hold her. They had left the gathering early, explaining that they had to pick up their daughter after her two-day visit with his family.

How many times had he gone over the circumstances in his mind? If only they had waited until the next day. If only he had seen the other car in time. If only he could have done something different! Then Andrea would be alive and here with him now.

His younger brother, Cody, couldn't let go of the fact that a hit-and-run driver had caused yet another fatal accident in the Callaway family. Fifteen years before Cameron and Andrea's accident, his mother and father had also been killed by one.

Cody was convinced that the two events were somehow linked. Cameron hadn't cared enough at the time to try to find out. Nothing could bring Andrea back to him. Nothing.

In the ensuing years, he had buried himself in his work. There was certainly enough to keep him busy. His older brother, Cole, was the head of Callaway Enterprises, which was a combination of real estate, oil and mineral interests, as well as various cattle businesses. Cameron was more than willing to let Cole run the show. He preferred to stay in the background, putting his degrees in accounting and law to work, being there whenever Cole needed him.

He walked through the familiar darkness of the bedroom that had been his since he was a child to the adjoining bathroom, where he flipped on the light. Its brilliance caused him to flinch. His sudden movement drew his eyes to the mirror and he caught a glimpse of himself. He shook his head in disgust. His blue eyes were swollen and rimmed with red. He rubbed his hand across his darkly stubbled jaw and chin. He looked ten years older than his thirty-four years. He felt more like sixty. His brown shaggy hair reminded him once again that he needed a haircut.

Reaching for the glass sitting beside the sink, he rinsed and filled it with water. After draining the contents, he flipped off the light and made his way back to bed.

He'd gone to bed around two in the morning. It was almost five now. His body ached with fatigue, but his mind continued to whir with too many thoughts to shut down.

He kept thinking about the trial he was in the middle of. All the evidence had been presented by Friday afternoon, and Cameron had hoped to go to summation on Monday morning, possibly turning the case over to the jurors by the afternoon. Unfortunately the judge had called a one-week recess because of previous commitments. Cameron felt caught in a state of frustrated limbo at the delay. He wanted to finish the case and get on with other pressing matters. But he had no choice now. Trial would resume when the judge said so. He might as well accept the situation.

Presentation had taken three weeks. He'd spent more than six months preparing for this one. He was determined to win. He was tired of Callaway Enterprises being made to look like a hungry conglomerate devouring smaller businesses. He and Cole had decided to plant their feet and fight back this time.

The battle was almost over, even though he had a week of enforced pause before beginning the next step in due process.

The Callaways were named in a number of lawsuits, either personally or as officers of various corporations. He supposed being the target of other people's ire came with the territory.

He and his brothers had inherited the family wealth when their parents were killed twenty years before. For more than seventy years the Callaway name had grown in prestige and power in Texas. With each succeeding generation, their companies had prospered and new companies had been formed.

He gave Cole the credit for most of the recent expansion. His brother had an uncanny knack for spotting trends of the future. He kept his businesses up-to-date, with state-of-the-art equipment in each one. He hired men who were brilliant strategists, willing to take responsibility, ready to stay at the forefront of the shifting and treacherous world of business.

Cole's business acumen was legendary.

Cameron, on the other hand, enjoyed the role of counselor and consultant to Cole. He couldn't have handled Cole's position. He didn't even want to try.

He sighed, consciously forcing his body to relax in a technique he had learned to reduce stress. He knew the stress of his heavy schedule wasn't making his life any easier. However, he preferred staying busy to having time—such as now, in the small hours of the night—to think, to remember, to grieve.

Slowly his body responded to his mental commands and Cameron managed to drift off to sleep once more.

He heard faint sounds in the distance and knew he needed to respond to them. They were persistent, no matter how much he tried to ignore them. He hated to move, though. He wanted to continue to drift in this netherworld, allowing himself to float away without thought or feeling. But the sounds wouldn't leave. They continued to call to him ...

"Daddy? Are you asleep? Daddy? Wake up, Daddy. There's a big lake out in front of the barn. You wanna see it, Daddy?"

Reluctantly, Cameron drifted upward, still longing for the oblivion of sleep. He could feel small hands patting both of his cheeks.

"Daddy? Wake up, Daddy," Trisha sang in a small soft voice.

His eyes felt swollen and glued shut. He forced them open, blinking. The first thing he saw was a pair of wide sherry-colored eyes staring back at him from a pixie-shaped face. As soon as his gaze met hers, she laughed in delight. "I knew you was awake! You was just playing possum, wasn't you, Daddy?"

He groaned. She was draped across his chest, her head bobbing in front of him.

"Trisha, sugar," he managed to say, "Daddy can't breathe very well when you lie on his chest like that."

Obligingly she began to slide down his body. Suddenly realizing what a five-year-old's weight would do to a full bladder, he woke up with a vengeance. Before she could continue moving, he lifted her off him and rolled so that they were side by side on the bed, facing each other.

"You know what, Daddy?" she asked, not missing a beat despite the sudden move.

"What, angel?"

"You missed breakfast."

He widened his eyes in simulated shock. "Really?"

She nodded vigorously. "An' you know what?"

He sighed. "What, baby?"

"Aunt Letty said it's 'bout time you showed up around here. She said—"

"You know something, sugar?" he interrupted, hugging her to him. "Your aunt Letty is a hundred percent right, as usual." He placed a kiss on her nose and she giggled.

"It stopped raining," Trisha said.

"Glad to hear it," he replied with heartfelt sincerity.

"Are you hungry?"

He couldn't remember the last time he'd eaten. He skipped more meals than he thought about eating.

"You bet," he said, more to be agreeable than honest.

Trisha gave him a heart-stopping smile. "Good, 'cause I helped Angie bake cookies this morning, and she says we gotta save you some."

"So why don't you run downstairs, darlin', while I shower, okay?"

"Okay." She slid away from him on her stomach, wriggling backward until she landed on her feet with a light bounce. "Hurry, Daddy." She dashed out of the room, slamming the door behind her.

He checked the time and discovered that it was almost eleven. When he had finally gotten to sleep he had been dead to the world. Yawning widely, he scratched his chest and rolled out of bed. Cookies, hmm. Angie knew he was particularly susceptible to her chocolate-chip cookies. He smiled to himself. It felt good to be home.

If Janine Talbot hadn't been determined to speak to Mr. Cameron Callaway today, she knew she never would have attempted this trip. Ever since she had left the highway, she had inched her car along a narrow blacktopped surface surrounded by water. At times the water ran across the road, causing her to stop. This was truly a case of come hell or high water, she intended to speak her mind to Mr. Callaway. She considered high water the better of the two choices.

She knew she was on the Circle C ranch. She had headed south from the town of Cielo, where she lived, knowing that the Callaway ranch was in that general direction. When she saw adobe pillars supporting an arching wrought-iron sign with a giant C in a circle, she knew she had found the ranch. Unfortunately, after she had driven under the sign, there was no indication that anyone or anything lived in these godforsaken hills. Other than water, she hadn't seen anything moving for what seemed like miles.

At least the rain had finally stopped. The weather forecast on the radio had been filled with warnings of flooding in outlying low areas. Surely the Callaway ranch was protected. From everything she had heard in the year since she had moved to Texas, the Callaways were a force to be reckoned with. No doubt they controlled wind, rain, fire and flooding with nonchalant ease.

A small elfin face flashed into her mind, and she found herself smiling, despite her unease about her unknown destination. Trisha Callaway. What a darling she was. Trisha had captured Janine's heart the first time Janine had seen the little girl and learned that she had lost her mother when she was barely a year old.

Trisha had been placed in Janine's preschool class a few weeks earlier. She had been shy with the other children at first, preferring to stay with the adults, Janine in particular. Janine had done everything she could think of to coax the little girl into playing with the others. After more than two weeks, she could see Trisha finally beginning to warm toward the other children.

Not that she was shy! Janine thought. Heavens, no. Trisha Callaway was a scamp. Janine knew that the little girl's family would be horrified if they had any idea of some of the things Trisha had told Janine. A recent conversation with Trisha came to mind, typical of their exchanges.

"My aunt Allison is going to have another baby, and she says the doctor told her there's going to be two at once! Won't that be neat? They already have a boy that's big and a girl that's littler 'n me, and Aunt Letty says she wonders if they ever get anything else done the way they're always huggin' and stuff. Do you know my aunt Allison?"

Janine bit her lip in an effort to hide her smile and shook her head.

"She's pretty. She's got long black hair that comes down to here." Trisha turned around and pointed to her buttocks. "She can sit on it!" she added with a giggle.

"Does she live with you?"

Trisha looked somber. "Not really. She and Uncle Cole come to visit when they can. They live in Austin. Tony goes to school there."

"Tony?"

"My cousin. He's big, even bigger than you."

"Really?" Janine responded. "Does your aunt Letty live with you?"

Trisha nodded solemnly. "Yes. Aunt Letty's always lived at the ranch, and she'll live there forever, Uncle Cody says, 'cause she's older 'n God!"

"I see," Janine said, nearly choking in an effort to stifle her laughter. "Does your uncle Cody live there, too?"

Trisha cocked her head for a moment, obviously giving the matter careful thought. "Sometimes he does, but most times he's gone off somewhere and nobody can find him. Aunt Letty says he's wild and up to no good, but I like him. He plays with me when he's home and answers all my questions and stuff like that."

"Does your daddy play with you?"

Trisha's face clouded. "When he's there. Most of the time he lives in San Antonio."

"San Antonio! That's more than an hour's drive from here."

Trisha nodded sagely. "Uh-huh. That's why he sleeps in town mostly. He comes to see me when he can." She looked down at her hands. "I miss him." She glanced back at Janine and said stoutly, "My daddy loves me and misses me a bunch."

"I'm sure he does, punkin. How could he not love someone as sweet as you?" She patted the little girl's shoulder with affection.

Maybe the man did love his daughter, Janine thought now as she carefully followed the wet winding road back through sagebrush, cactus and mesquite, but he wasn't paying much attention to her—otherwise, he would see that she was not happy and know that she was having difficulty in adjusting to preschool.

The child was too well mannered to cry when she was brought to the school each morning by one of the ranch employees, but her woebegone face was a clear indicator of how she felt.

For the past week she had barely touched the midmorning snack the school supplied. True, she was a small-boned child. However, Janine couldn't help but wonder if Trisha was eating enough. The child was obviously unhappy about something, and when Janine had asked her the morning before if something was wrong, tears came to the child's eyes and slowly rolled down her cheeks. "I want my daddy," she whispered.

"Oh, honey, I know you do. Have you talked to him?"

She nodded her head. "He promised he'd come to see me this weekend, and he never breaks a promise, but Aunt Letty said she didn't care if he promised to come or not, even a idiot would know better than to drive out here in this weather."

"Maybe he'll make it, anyway," Janine had said in an effort to console her small charge.

"You think so?"

Janine had closed her eyes in a brief prayer. She had wished she knew the man better. Did he understand the importance of keeping a promise to a child? She had known then that she was going to have to do something about Trisha. No matter how many times she had reminded herself not to get emotionally involved with her students, she knew that this particular child had slipped past all the barriers around her heart.

When she had awakened that morning, she knew she was going to drive to the ranch. If Trisha's father hadn't come, at least *she* would be there to cheer up the little girl. If he *was* there, well, then she would talk to him.

Now that she was within a few miles of him, Janine began to feel butterflies fluttering in her stomach. She wasn't exactly sure what she was going to say to him. Of course she knew what she *wanted* to say, but she would have to word her comments very carefully. Not that she was afraid of him or even intimidated by the

fact that he was a Callaway, but she didn't want to
make him angry if she could prevent it.

Let's face it, she told herself. *You're meddling and
you know it.* She'd spent hours trying to talk herself
out of coming, but in the end, she knew she had to do
everything she could to help remove that terrible look
of longing and sadness from Trisha's face.

"Oh my God!" She pressed down hard on the
brakes, jerked back to the present by the swollen creek
racing through a gully. A wooden bridge spanned it,
but the water was slithering over its sides and swirling
across the top. Maybe she should turn around and
come back some other time.

She looked up at the heavy clouds, which seemed so
low they appeared to be touching some of the taller
trees in the area. Surely she was almost there! Chas-
tising herself for being a coward, Janine eased her car
down the hill and onto the bridge, creeping forward
until she reached the other side.

She hadn't been aware she was holding her breath
until she finally let it go with a *whoosh.* She still hadn't
adjusted to Texas. Everything was bigger and better
and higher and deeper in Texas than anywhere else, to
hear the natives tell it. Colorado could have some
rough storms, particularly in the mountains, but she
would have to give Texas its due. When it decided to
rain and storm here, the results were tumultuous.

She reached the top of the incline and released another sigh of relief. There, in the hollow of the hills
below her, was one of the most beautiful sights she had
seen in south Texas.

A rambling multistoried house made of adobe and
whitewashed a gleaming white with a Spanish-tile roof

sat in the middle of a group of buildings; the place looked like a small village. A high wall encircled the compound, with an arched opening for the road she was on.

There were barns and paddocks, some with horses, others with cattle. There wasn't much sign of activity, only a few men around one of the barns.

Well! She had made it. Janine started down the winding road. She still had a distance to go, but at least she could see her destination.

By the time she drew up in front of a massive wooden door and turned off the car, she was trembling with exhaustion. She hadn't realized how tense she had been on that drive until now, when she knew she was safe. She sat for a moment, drawing deep breaths and reminding herself that she was there for Trisha's sake.

She checked in the mirror to make sure her reddish-brown hair was still tucked in a coil on the nape of her neck. Her green eyes reflected her apprehension. Darn! She wished her face didn't instantly signal her every emotion. She had long since learned not to play any games where a stoic expression counted.

"Come on," she muttered to herself, opening the car door. "You can do it. Just think of Trisha."

She stepped out and brushed the skirt of her yellow suit. She had deliberately chosen something bright on this gloomy day—to give herself courage, if nothing else. Had she mentioned her intentions to any of the other staff members, they would have been shocked that she would consider confronting one of the Callaways—which was exactly why she hadn't told anyone of her plans. Perhaps she could mention to them that she had happened to be passing by. She glanced around and realized that nobody could be just passing by this place. It had taken her almost half an hour to drive the private road from the highway.

So! She would go back to her original plan. If Cameron Callaway had decided to show up this weekend, she would meet him. She would explain who she was, and depending on his response, she would decide how to broach the purpose of her visit.

There. She felt better, now that she had mentally prepared herself for the next few moments. After gripping her purse, Janine walked to the front door and knocked.

A moment later, the door was opened by a young Hispanic woman with a pleasant face. "Hello. May I help you?"

From somewhere in the looming foyer behind the woman, Janine heard a gruff male voice say, "Who is it, Rosie?"

Janine cleared her throat before stating, "I came to see Mr. Cameron Callaway."

Rosie opened the door wider and motioned for Janine to come inside. With a wave of her arm Rosie indicated the man on the stairway.

Janine caught her breath. *Please, God. Please don't let this be the man I came to see.*

The first thing she noticed was his height. He was tall and broad-shouldered, with a lean waist and hips and long muscular legs. Then she noticed that he was only half-dressed. He wore a pair of faded jeans that looked as though they had been sewn on him. They hung low on his hips, the fly button left undone. Other than a pair of dilapidated moccasins on his feet, that was all the man wore.

As he moved down the stairs, she stared at the crisp curls that covered his chest. She barely noticed the blue chambray shirt clutched in one fist. When her gaze finally lifted she saw a pair of blazing blue eyes staring at her with a mixture of irritation and curiosity.

He needed a shave. The dark stubble on his jaw and chin made him look like some desperado from an earlier era. All he needed was a six-gun on his hip. His hair looked damp, as though he had just come from the shower. Although he had obviously combed it back from his face, a stray lock had fallen across his forehead.

"I'm Cameron Callaway. What can I do for you?"

Put on some clothes, was her first thought. Then she tried to get a grip on herself. "I, uh, was wondering if I could speak with you," she managed to say with a tongue that felt foreign to her mouth.

He moved on down the stairs and paused beside her. She had to tilt her head to continue to meet his eyes. He seemed to be taking inventory of her. That knowledge caused her to stiffen her spine. "I know I should have called first, but I thought I'd take a chance on catching you at home."

He studied her for a moment in silence before saying, "You were lucky to find me here. This is the first time I've been home in three weeks."

This was worse than she had thought. "Three weeks! But that's awful!" she blurted out, thinking of Trisha. No wonder the little girl had missed him.

He raised a brow slightly, looking puzzled. "Awful? That isn't the word that first comes to mind, but if you say so, I suppose it will do."

Janine could feel herself blushing. How she hated her fair skin and her annoying inclination to turn colors with the least amount of provocation.

He shook out his shirt and slid his arms into it, rolling the sleeves while he left his chest bare. Determined not to stare, Janine glanced around. They stood in a large foyer. The ceiling was more than two stories high. The red Spanish tile of the floor gleamed. Toward the back she could see a glass door that framed an inner courtyard filled with a profusion of flowers and a fountain.

When she glanced back at the man beside her, his shirt was buttoned about midway down his chest, but the tails hung out. He motioned her through one of the arched doorways. "I just got up and I really need a cup of coffee. I'm afraid I use coffee to help me become civilized," he said with a slight smile. "Care to join me?"

She tried to hide her disapproval. It was almost noon, for heaven's sake. But at least he appeared amiable enough. For some reason she felt as though she had approached a lion in his lair. At the moment he was groggy and not particularly aware of her, but she had a hunch he could focus his attention rapidly with a laserlike gaze.

"Rosie, set another place for..." He glanced at her and said, "I'm sorry. I forgot to ask your name."

"Oh!" She had neglected to introduce herself. "I'm, uh, Janine Talbot. I live in Cielo. I came to talk to you about Trisha."

"Oh? Well, have a seat."

Janine found the massive table with its long row of chairs almost intimidating. Place settings were at one end of the table. After pouring their coffee, Rosie smiled at her and disappeared into what Janine supposed was the kitchen.

Cameron sat down, picked up his cup and took a sip. He gave a sigh of pleasure before taking another sip.

Janine wasn't certain why he seemed so much more male to her than the other men she knew, but he did. He also made her very aware of herself as a female.

"How do you know my daughter?" he asked after he finished his first cup and poured himself another one. He reached over to refill her cup, then paused, when he noted that she still had most of a cup left.

"She's one of my students," she said, wondering how to begin the conversation now that she was face-to-face with the man.

He stared at her. "One of your what?"

"My students."

"What do you teach to a five-year-old?"

She stared at him in astonishment. "We have a schedule of various activities, which I could go over with you, if you'd like. The preschool is quite—"

"Preschool! Are you telling me that Trisha is attending a preschool in Cielo?"

"Well, yes. I thought you knew."

He closed his eyes and massaged the bridge of his nose with his fingers. "Letty's at it again," he muttered.

She wasn't certain that she heard him correctly. "I beg your pardon?"

He dropped his hand wearily and sighed. "Nothing. Go on. So you have Trisha in your class." The last thing he needed right after getting out of bed in the morning was a parent-teacher conference about his daughter.

She clasped her hands in her lap. "Yes. And she doesn't seem to be very happy."

"I'm not surprised. I could have told that to you or Letty or whoever thought Trisha should be carted off to school. She hates to be penned up... and she's not scheduled to start school until the fall. She should be out running and playing like the rest of the five-year-olds."

Janine warned herself not to become defensive. If he hadn't been in contact with his daughter for three weeks, it was no wonder the child was so lonely. Her heart ached for the neglected little girl. Choosing her words carefully and attempting a neutral tone, she replied, "Well, actually, we do have plenty of recreational time for the children. The problem is, Trisha refuses to join them."

He took a sip of his coffee before saying, "That's Trisha for you. She's definitely got a mind of her own."

"It's obvious that she's not used to being around children her own age. She's not at all happy there. She prefers staying inside and talking with me. That's why we felt she should spend this semester at the school."

"Then the obvious solution is for her not to go. I don't understand what Letty was thinking about in the first place. I'll have to talk to her." As far as Cameron was concerned, the discussion had come to an end.

If Trisha didn't like preschool, then she didn't have to go.

"We keep hoping she will adapt to being around children her own age," Janine said. "By going to school now, she will have an easier time of adjustment when she begins kindergarten in the fall."

He didn't respond to her comment. Instead, he shoved his fingers through his hair in a frustrated movement, rumpling the combed appearance into unruly waves, and frowned.

She placed her clasped hands on the table and leaned forward. "Mr. Callaway, I think she's upset about more than going to school, which is why I decided to come to see you today."

He lifted his gaze to hers, and she felt pinned to her chair by its intensity.

"I'm glad we're getting to the point of all of this. What do you think is the problem?"

This discussion was much tougher than she had anticipated. Cameron Callaway was nothing like the man she had pictured while listening to Trisha's stories over the past few weeks. He was much harder, for one thing. The longer she was in his company, the more nervous she became. She cleared her throat. "Are you aware of how much your daughter misses you? She talks about you all the time."

He sat back in his chair and grinned at her. She hadn't been prepared for the sudden glimpse of the charming and very attractive side of the man. She found him quite disconcerting.

"Well, I miss her, too. We don't seem to have much time togeth—" He stopped and stared at her. "Is this what your visit is all about? You drove all the way out here just to tell me that my daughter misses me?''

She could feel her cheeks turning red again. ''Well, you see, I—''

''Or did you come out here to tell me that I'm neglecting my daughter, that I don't spend enough time with her, that I...'' He shoved back his chair and stood. So did she. ''Look, Ms. Talbot, I don't need some prim and proper schoolmarm to tell me how to raise my own child.'' The look he gave her would have melted steel at ten paces. ''If Trisha isn't happy at school, then let her stay home. If she misses me, then I'll take care of it. I don't want someone like you, who doesn't know a damn thing about raising kids, to give me advice!'' He seldom lost control of his temper but the combination of overwork, lack of sleep and lack of proper meals had pushed him beyond his normal self-control.

He placed his hands on the table and leaned on them, glaring at her. In a low voice shaking with intensity, he said, ''The problem with you, lady, is that you obviously have too damn much time on your hands. I would guess that teaching school is your life. Well, you drove all the way out here to give me the benefit of your advice. I wouldn't want you to go away empty-handed, so I've got some advice for you. Why don't you get married and have your *own* family and quit worrying so much about mine!''

By the time he finished speaking Janine was already at the door to the hallway. She was shaking with indignation and anger, but she refused to allow the man to have the last word. She turned and looked at him, standing there glaring at her from the end of the table as though he was at a board of directors' meeting. Perhaps his manner quelled his opposition in the business world, but she was not going to let it quell her!

She braced her shoulders and with her chin high, responded, "At least now I better understand why your daughter is the way she is. I feel sorry for you, Mr. Callaway, I really do. With all your wealth and power, you haven't recognized what you have. You have been given a priceless jewel and you don't even understand her value. I feel even sorrier for Trisha, however. Unfortunately she can't move to another family who might have more time for her, a family that would nurture her and make her feel secure. She has no choice but to stay here and emotionally wither away!" She spun on her heel and marched out of his sight.

Cameron sat back down in his chair with a thump and stared at the empty doorway where the young woman with the flaming temper had been standing just a moment ago. He heard the front door slam with a resounding crash. A few seconds later, he heard an engine rev and the sound of tires peeling out.

Trisha chose that moment to come tearing into the dining room. "Daddy, Daddy! You're up, you're up!" She threw herself into his lap and he absently hugged her to him. His daughter? Emotionally withering?

"Angie said I could ask you what you want to eat."

"Anything. I don't care."

"You want breakfast or lunch?"

"Breakfast."

She threw herself out of his arms and raced to the kitchen door. "I'll tell her."

Withering? Any more energy and the house wouldn't contain her.

He sat there in the large room by himself, feeling ashamed. He usually kept a tight rein on his temper. He had been provoked by much more scathing critics before and hadn't allowed himself to be affected. But somehow this was different. She had attacked him in the most vulnerable area of his life.

She had immediately zeroed in on his weakest point, recognizing his lack of parenting skills. He was aware of his shortcomings. He just didn't know what to do about them. His intentions had been good. He had never intended to go so long without being with Trisha, and had hoped the daily telephone calls had made a difference.

Who was he kidding? He hadn't even known something as important as his daughter, his only child, being enrolled in school.

Why hadn't Trisha mentioned it to him when they talked? She went to great lengths describing a frog or a television cartoon, but hadn't mentioned how she had been spending her weekday mornings.

The mystery of what went on in a child's mind continued to elude him.

Who was this Janine Talbot? He thought he knew most of the people in Cielo. He had grown up in this neck of the woods. He had attended the local schools, but he sure as hell didn't know her. He would have remembered. How could anyone forget those green eyes, filled with accusations? Beneath the chandelier her dark brown hair had glowed with red highlights. She had definitely brightened the day in her saucy yellow suit, which set off a great pair of legs. The rest of her figure was nothing to sneeze at, either. He cringed when he remembered some of the things he had said to her and knew that he would have to look her up and offer her an apology. That was the least he could do.

He reached over and poured himself another cup of coffee.

So why *wasn't* she married with a house full of kids? He had noticed that she wasn't wearing any rings. Not that it mattered to him.

He wasn't interested in anyone and didn't intend to be. He would never go through the pain of falling in love and possibly losing that love again. Not ever. At least he had Trisha. Despite Ms. Talbot's accusations, he did love his daughter, very much. He wanted the very best for her.

Rosie brought him his breakfast. He thoroughly enjoyed every bite, feeling almost mellow by the time she came in to remove the dirty dishes.

He decided to go find Letty and talk to her. Since the solarium was his aunt's favorite room, rain or shine, he would start there. He had just stepped into the hallway when he heard a pounding at the front door.

"I'll get it, Rosie," he said, and opened the door. His mouth fell open in shock.

The rain coming down in buckets must have started since he had come downstairs. This was the rainy season, so there was nothing shocking in that discovery. The shock was seeing Janine Talbot on his front doorstep once again, soaking wet. She was trembling.

Already ashamed of his earlier outburst he took her arm wordlessly and gently pulled her inside, where she stood, dripping. Tiny rivers of water began to snake across the floor. Her once immaculate suit was now mud-spattered and clung to her body, confirming his earlier assessment of her figure. There were certainly no flaws there.

Her hair hung in several long ropes around her shoulders, each one dripping. She shoved some wisps off her forehead and stared at him helplessly.

"What happened? Did you wreck your car? Are you all right?"

She shivered, then wrapped her arms around herself. "I... Your bridge... When I got to the first bridge I couldn't believe it. It's gone!"

"What? The bridge is gone?"

She nodded. "I got out of the car and walked down to the water. There was just nothing there. I didn't know what to do." She glanced up at him, then quickly away. "I didn't want to come back here. I was just standing there, staring at all the water, when suddenly the rain started again without warning. I felt as though I was standing beneath a rushing waterfall." She glanced down at herself and moaned. "I couldn't think of anything else to do, so I came back."

Obviously the drenching had cooled her off a bit, but he didn't consider it polite to point that out just then.

"Look, you need to get out of those wet clothes. And we need to talk. I owe you an apology for blowing up at you like that. What I said was really unforgivable, I know. It's just been a bear of a week all the way around. I shouldn't have taken it out on you, though."

He placed his hand on her back. If anything, the shivering increased. "Let's get you upstairs and dried off, okay?"

Janine closed her eyes, trying to think. The whole morning had been an unmitigated disaster. When she had left this man earlier she had vowed never to see him again. Now she was in a position where she had little choice but to accept his help.

How demoralizing.

Nothing so embarrassing, so potentially humiliating, had happened to her in her thirty-two years. For the first time since she had moved to Texas, she wondered if she had made a mistake. Perhaps she should have stayed in Colorado, after all.

Two

Once again Cameron urged her forward. Janine realized there was nothing for her to do but go with him. She couldn't continue to stand there in the hallway and watch the rivulets of water form liquid patterns on the highly glossed tiles.

He removed his hand from her back once he saw she was willing to follow him up the stairs. Janine stayed a couple of steps behind, looking around at her surroundings.

She had never had a particular curiosity about the Callaways, and that had made her a definite minority at the private school where she had been teaching for a little more than a year. She still remembered the flurry of excitement when a member of the new generation of the Callaway family had begun attending the school. She had been amazed at her fellow workers' eagerness to learn anything they could about Trisha and her family.

She could well imagine the questions she would receive when she told them of this latest mishap of hers. She was known for her mishaps. If anyone had a problem with any of the school equipment, it invariably was her.

Once she had inadvertently locked herself in her classroom, something no one had thought about when a particular style of locks had been placed on the doors. She had left the building for the day when she suddenly remembered some papers she needed. Leaving her purse in the car, she'd dashed back into the school and unlocked her door, leaving her keys in the lock. It never occurred to her to brace the door. When some other door was opened in the building, the ensuing draft sucked her classroom door shut and there she was, locked in.

Thank God someone had heard her banging on the door. The louvered windows would have been next to impossible to crawl out of. Nobody since had ever allowed her to forget the incident!

Now she told herself to try to remember everything she saw. Perhaps a detailed description of the place would satisfy their curiosity when she was questioned about her visit. Maybe no one would have to know that she had ended up being trapped at the Callaway ranch.

There were three hallways leading off the balcony overlooking the foyer below. Cameron started down the center one. She hurried behind him, aware of the squishing noise her shoes made with each step. Her beautiful, almost new shoes were totally ruined. At the moment they were the least of her worries.

Cameron paused in front of a door. "Excuse the mess. I'm going to let you get out of those sodden clothes. You can shower here in my room. Meantime, I'll look to see what Allison has here that you can wear."

"Allison?"

"My brother Cole's wife. They live in Austin, but they spend as much of their time as possible here at the ranch. They keep clothes here for when they come down." He held the door open and waved her through, then closed it behind him, leaving her alone.

Janine stood in front of the closed door and gazed around at the masculine bedroom. The twisted bedclothes gave mute evidence that he had spent a restless night. A suit jacket and pants were tossed over the back of a comfortable-looking chair positioned in front of a fireplace.

Remembering that she was now leaving soggy tracks in the plush carpeting, Janine hurried over to the open doorway of the bathroom. Wisps of steam seemed to linger in the room. She shivered, feeling the coldness of her damp clothes seep through to her bones. With shaking fingers, she peeled off her jacket and gazed at it with sorrow. This suit was one of her very favorites, and the children loved it. She sighed. Perhaps the cleaners would be able to salvage it. She carefully draped it across the clothes hamper, then slipped out of her blouse and skirt. Even her slip and underclothes were damp.

As soon as the hot water from the shower hit her chilled body, she groaned with relief. She couldn't remember when anything had felt so good. She stuck her head under the water and massaged her scalp. Heaven. Absolute heaven.

By the time Janine stepped out of the shower, she felt like a new person. She found an oversize thick towel that enveloped her from her shoulders to her knees and began to dry off, leaving her skin looking rosy.

A soft tap on the bathroom door startled her so much she almost dropped the towel. "Yes?" she asked, grabbing the slipping cloth.

"I found one of Allison's lounging robes for you. It's on the bed," she heard Cameron say.

"Fine," she managed to reply in a calm tone, which covered the quavering feelings this man managed to evoke. She wasn't certain exactly why. Of course he was a Callaway, and that was intimidating enough, right there. But it was more than that. He caused a reaction in her that she couldn't understand. She was embarrassed by the fact that she had lost her temper with him. She couldn't have been more unprofessional if she had tried. His comments had upset her because he had been right. The school and her job *were* her life. Most of her friends were coworkers there.

He had called her prim and proper. Was that how she appeared to him?

Janine glanced into the mirror, which was slowly clearing from the steam of her shower. The towel left her shoulders bare. Her freshly shampooed hair was already beginning to dry and to bounce into waves and curls. The only way she could keep it straight and tidy

was to blow-dry her hair immediately after shampoo-
ing.

Searching around for a hand-held drier seemed a
little too nosy, so she would have to allow her hair to
dry naturally.

She leaned toward the mirror. Prim and proper. Did
it show so plainly? Her wide green eyes gazed back at
her. Was it the way she dressed or wore her hair or her
makeup? Maybe it was her clothes. What gave her
away?

She felt that she had made the very best life she
could make in her circumstances. She loved children
and therefore had decided to devote her life to them,
even if they weren't hers. Did the children see her as
prim?

Her mind flashed back to a time earlier in the week
when she had been down on the floor with her class,
taking her turn at pretending to be a chicken—flap-
ping her wings, shaking her neck, pecking at grain on
the floor.

Or the time she had brought in a life-size papier-
mâché turtle's shell and proceeded to climb under it to
demonstrate the difficulties in carrying your home
around on your back. The children had loved it. She
wondered what Trisha's father would have thought of
her lying on her back attempting to flip herself over.

She gave her hair a final toweling, then peeked
around the bathroom door to make certain he had left.
The room was empty. She tiptoed out and then
laughed at herself. Why was she trying to be quiet? In
a house this size a party could be going on in one wing
and few would hear it in the other, she was certain.

The lounging robe on the bed was absolutely gorgeous. Never had she felt material so soft. The colors were a swirl of blue and green with brief touches of gold. Obviously Allison Callaway had a marvelous eye for color, texture and style. She found a note beside the robe that read, "I wasn't sure of your shoe size. Here's a pair of my socks for now." A big "C" was scrawled at the bottom. His handwriting was bold, slashing across the page.

He was being very genial, considering the way they had parted earlier. She couldn't believe how she had behaved, which was totally out of character. There was just something about that man that made her feel— and act—in a way she couldn't understand.

After she slipped on the robe and socks, she returned to the bathroom and draped her clothes over the various rods, in the vague hope they would dry sometime soon. Then she returned to the bedroom and peeked out the window.

Rain continued to fall, setting up a syncopated rhythm as it hit the panes of glass. She smiled. If her students were there she would have them listen very carefully to see if they could recognize a tune.

By the time she had brushed her hair a few times with the small brush she carried in her purse, she knew she was as ready as she would ever be to find Cameron Callaway. He had been gracious with his apology. She could be no less.

She realized as soon as she stepped into the hallway that she wasn't sure how to find her way back downstairs. Which direction had they come from? She looked both ways and saw nothing that seemed familiar, despite her earlier efforts to remember details.

Hesitantly she turned left and started down the hallway. When it ended, she was standing on the balcony overlooking the foyer, and she allowed herself a quick sigh of relief.

So far, so good.

She came downstairs and noted that the puddle of water by the front door had already been mopped up. The floor looked as polished as ever, thank goodness. She wandered toward the back, glancing into opened doors and wondering what she was supposed to do now.

"Missy Talbot! You came to see me!"

She spun around in time to catch a human dynamo as Trisha shot out of one of the rooms and grabbed her around the knees, almost toppling her.

"Hi, Trisha!"

"Oh, Missy Talbot. I didn't know you knew where I live. Do you want to see where I play?"

Janine immediately felt more comfortable now that she was with the little girl. "Sure, Trisha. Lead the way."

The room they entered was a child's fairyland. Three sides were glass, as was most of the roof. It jutted into the interior courtyard so that the fountain and flowers seemed to be a part of the room.

Inside, comfortably padded rattan furniture took up part of the space while the rest was devoted to toys and games. A miniature child's kitchen was in one area, complete with tiny dishes, as well as pots and pans.

An old-fashioned rocking horse sat in another corner.

Hanging baskets hung from various supports, adding color and greenery to the room.

"This is marvelous, Trisha. I bet you have lots of fun."

"Uh-huh, but it's more fun when Katie comes to visit."

"Is Katie one of your friends?"

"Uh-huh. She's my cousin. That's kinda like a sister, but she lives with her own mommy and daddy. Her mommy's going to have two more babies sometime."

"Ah, I remember now. Katie must be your aunt Allison's little girl."

"She's littler than me. She's only two and a half. She brings her baby dolls and we play like we're mommies."

Janine felt a lump form in her throat at the reminder of how young the urge to have a baby begins. She swallowed painfully. "I see."

"Do you want to see my dolls?"

She sank into one of the chairs, nodding.

Trisha spun away and went over to a line of tiny beds. She first picked up one doll, then another, until her hands were full. She returned to Janine and placed them on her lap. "Aren't they pretty?" she whispered, leaning against Janine's knee.

Each doll showed the results of being well loved, although their gowns were clean and well kept. Janine stared down at the blond-headed little girl and wanted to weep. She had obviously been giving her dolls the love and the nurturing that she, herself, wanted from a mother. Was there anyone in her life who gave that to her?

"Trisha, it's time for your lunch and then nap time." Janine glanced around and saw a tall thin woman with gray hair standing in the doorway. The woman nodded to Janine. "You must be Ms. Talbot. I'm Letitia Callaway, Cameron's aunt. Cameron said you had stopped in to see him this morning. We must apologize for the inconvenience of the bridge. You were very fortunate not to have been on it when it was swept away."

Janine hadn't considered that gruesome thought. She shuddered inwardly.

"Cameron's out with the men now," Letty went on, "checking the damage all this water has done. Would you like to have lunch with Trisha?"

"Oh, yes!" Trisha replied, clapping her hands. "We could have a tea party."

The older woman's face softened for a moment. Janine wondered if she ever smiled. The lines in her face seemed permanent, as though she seldom changed expression. "That might be nice," Letty conceded, glancing at Janine for confirmation.

"Oh, whatever is convenient for you. I'm so sorry to have gotten stranded here like this. I had hoped when I left home this morning that the bad weather was over." She helped Trisha return the dolls to their respective beds and followed the older woman out of the room.

They arrived in a small room that looked like a breakfast nook, nothing as grand as the large dining room where Cameron had taken her earlier. Rosie was placing food on the table when they walked in. She smiled and left the room. Janine noted there were only two places set.

"Aren't you going to join us?" she asked Cameron's aunt.

"No. I don't eat much during the day. None of us keep regular schedules around here until evening, when we make it a point to gather for dinner at seven." She glanced at the robe Janine wore. "You're about the same size as Allison. She won't mind if you borrow more of her clothes."

"Oh, surely I'll be able to get home soon."

The woman just looked at her. "Don't count on it. It won't be the first time we've been marooned here. I'm sure it won't be the last."

"Oh, but—" She stopped talking when she realized the woman wasn't staying to hear anything she might say. The door swung shut behind her.

"I'm so glad you're here to eat with me," Trisha said. "It gets lonesome eating by myself."

"Do you always eat alone?"

"Sometimes I pretend Daddy is here. Sometimes my pretend friend stays to eat."

"Your pretend friend?"

"Ralph. He's a giant who used to live in the hills, but he's scared of the dark so I invited him to stay with me."

"I see. And he agreed?"

"Most of the time. Sometimes he goes and checks on things, like giants have to do."

By the time they finished their meal, Trisha's head was nodding. It took little effort for Janine to convince her to go lie down for her nap, especially after she promised to be there when Trisha woke up.

Janine stayed with her until she fell asleep, more aware than ever of what a lonely existence the child had. Perhaps she had been out of line talking to the girl's father, but she had done it out of love and concern for Trisha. Her heart ached for her, but she knew that she could say no more. She had already done enough damage.

When Cameron returned to the house, he was wet, cold and disgusted. There wasn't a damn thing anyone was going to be able to do until the rain let up and the water slowed down. There was no sense in risking someone's drowning in an attempt to reestablish a connection to the main highway.

He had discussed the matter with Alejandro, the ranch foreman, who assured him that he would keep an eye on the flooding creek. As soon as it was feasible, he would get the men working on something to provide temporary access, until the family could get the bridge rebuilt.

Cameron had come into the house in the back way. On his way upstairs to change clothes, he glanced into the family room and saw Janine sitting curled up at the end of the couch in front of a crackling fire, glancing through a magazine.

He had trouble recognizing the woman as the same one who had arrived that morning. With her hair down and curling around her face, she looked considerably younger. The flickering flames highlighted the burnished red of her hair. She looked as though she belonged there, waiting for him to come home. Cameron had an almost irresistible urge to walk in, stretch out on the couch and put his head in her lap. He could almost feel her long slender fingers stroking through his hair and along his jaw.

When he realized where his thoughts were leading him, he silently cursed and spun on his heel, heading toward the stairs.

He had been too long without a woman, that was all. He wasn't yearning for a relationship, no matter how his thoughts betrayed him.

He took the stairs two at a time, pulling at the snaps on his shirt. What a mess. There was no way to get rid of her. He supposed he could contact Pete in San Antonio and have him pick her up in the company helicopter, but what reason could he give? The situation wasn't an emergency, by any means. Surely by Monday the water would have gone down enough to rig up something to use temporarily to get across the creek. Besides, there was no sense risking a flight in this kind of weather.

He glanced out the window of his room. The rain continued to beat down. Alejandro had told him that he had most of the crew moving cattle from low-lying areas up into the hills. That was more important than the bridge. Hell, this place was like a town. They had enough provisions at the ranch to take care of those who lived there for weeks.

The shower felt good, and Cameron allowed his mind to go blank as he stood beneath the soothing spray. His thoughts drifted back to Janine Talbot.

They were both stranded for the time being. With his case in recess for the next week, he had intended to catch up on correspondence and other work at the office. He supposed he could have his secretary fax him whatever needed to be taken care of immediately.

In the meantime, he and Ms. Talbot would be forced to tolerate each other.

Her sudden outburst of temper had surprised him. She had seemed very calm and quiet when they had first spoken. Obviously he had touched a nerve.

Well, hell. So had she. Who did she think she was, coming in here and telling him he was neglecting his child?

He sighed. Damn. He knew she was right. Even though he spoke to Trisha every day, he had not seen her for weeks.

His biggest problem was that he knew so little about children. He was doing the best he could. So why did the woman's green eyes keep popping into his head, staring at him in silent reproach?

He turned off the water faucet and stepped out of the shower. Grabbing a towel, he rubbed his head and body vigorously, then tossed it onto the clothes hamper and—

How had he missed the fact that her clothes were hanging here in his bathroom? He stared around him. Her jacket, blouse, skirt, slip and the laciest bra and pair of briefs he'd ever seen were draped everywhere.

He felt as though he had received a punch just below the heart. Visions of life with Andrea crowded into his mind. He had been alone for four years. In that time he had forgotten what it was like to have feminine apparel around him. He also had forgotten how much he had enjoyed sharing space with someone he loved.

He closed his eyes, waiting for the sudden rush of pain to subside once again.

Cole and Cody had assured him that he would get over feeling so much anguish. They had pointed to the horrible time in their lives when they lost their parents. They had learned to live with tragedy. What Cameron realized was that a person never stopped feeling the ache of loss; he just grew used to living with it.

Something would trigger a memory and he would travel back in time and be with Andrea before he could control the sudden mental leap. When he was told she was dead, he had wanted to die, too. His brothers had later told him that the doctors had been worried about his recovery once he had learned Andrea was gone.

Didn't anyone understand that he hadn't cared whether he lived or died? He hadn't known how he could go on without Andrea.

But he had. He had made it by dealing with each day as it came and never looking too far ahead. He couldn't bear to think about the future and know that Andrea wasn't going to be there when Trisha grew older. They had talked about what it would feel like to send her off to school for the first time. They had talked about having other children, so Trisha wouldn't grow up alone.

None of that seemed to matter anymore. Trisha was growing up alone, and he hadn't even known when she had started school.

By the time Cameron came downstairs, he had pushed all the memories away, forcing himself once again to concentrate on the present. When he walked into the family room, he was again shaken by the scene he found there. Janine had discarded the magazine she had been reading and had leaned her head against the couch. Her eyes were closed, and Cameron wasn't certain whether she was asleep or just resting.

Moving silently past her, he added a couple of small logs to the fire, rearranging what was left. When he finished he stood and turned. Although she hadn't moved her position, her eyes were open.

"I didn't mean to disturb you," he said.

"You didn't. I was, uh, waiting to see you, to thank you for looking after me so well and to..." She paused and took a deep breath before continuing, "And to apologize for my behavior earlier. I was totally out of line and I'm sorry. I should never have said those things to you."

He nodded, then looked away as though uncomfortable with her apology. When he looked back at her, they just stared at each other without speaking. Finally Janine asked, "Were you able to do anything about the bridge?"

He shook his head. "I'm afraid we're both stuck here for a while yet."

She raised her head. "Both?"

"Yes. I had planned to return to San Antonio tomorrow. I've been in trial for the past three weeks. Although we have a one-week recess, there are several matters I need to deal with at the office. Now I'll have to deal with them from here the best way I can."

"You're an attorney?"

"Yes. I thought you knew."

She shook her head, and her hair flowed around her shoulders. "No. I don't think Trisha understands exactly what it is you do," she added with a smile.

He didn't return the smile. "I assumed you had other sources than Trisha."

She raised her chin slightly, her gaze never leaving his. "If you're insinuating that I've been prying into your family's affairs, Mr. Callaway, then you're wrong. I know very little about any of you."

He allowed himself a brief smile of acknowledgment. "I wasn't insinuating anything, Ms. Talbot. It has been my experience that for some reason the media finds our family fascinating. Almost everything any one of us does gets mentioned in newspapers, magazines or the television news. It would be difficult not to know anything about us."

"Oh. Then I must appear to be grossly uninformed. I only moved to Texas a year ago. Either the Callaways have been unnewsworthy during that time, or I must have missed catching sight of you on the six-o'clock news reports!"

He grinned at her tart tone and sat down at the other end of the couch. "Where are you from?"

"Colorado."

"Ah. Beautiful country. What caused you to move to Texas?"

"I was offered the position I now hold here. I'd decided to get away from the area where I grew up. I wanted to start over somewhere else once my mother died. I wanted to make new friends and enjoy a new life."

He heard an edge in her voice that didn't seem to fit in with the information she was readily offering him. All of it sounded innocuous enough on the surface, but there were brief hints of some buried emotion. Pain?

"I wouldn't expect Cielo to be the kind of town that would draw a person away from the spectacular beauty of your home state. The last I heard, the population of Cielo was about twenty-five thousand people."

"I like it."

"Glad to hear it."

Once again a silence enfolded them. When he saw that she wasn't going to say anything more, he spoke. "I want you to know that I really am sorry for what I said to you earlier. The truth is that I'm aware I don't spend enough time with Trisha, and I'm a little sensitive about it. Added to that is the fact that Letty didn't bother to tell me she was putting her in preschool. I didn't expect her to be going to school until next fall."

"When she came in this spring for testing, we felt that she needed to learn how to be around children her own age. The head of the school discussed the matter with someone in your family. I assumed it was you, Mr. Callaway. It was agreed that she would start attending classes this spring."

Cameron leaned forward, rested his elbows on his knees and ran one of his hands through his hair, his gaze on the floor. "No," he said wearily, "it wasn't me."

"She loves you very much, you know," he heard her say softly. Why didn't that make him feel any better?

"And I adore her, but I know that she hasn't seen many signs of that."

Once again she was silent, and Cameron felt the silence condemning him. Slowly he straightened, then turned and held her gaze. "Look, since we've been thrown together for the next few days, why don't we dispense with the formality. My name is Cameron. My friends and family call me Cam."

He looked so uncomfortably earnest that she smiled. "I'm Janine."

"Janine. That's very pretty."

"Thank you."

"Does the rest of your family still live in Colorado?"

She shook her head. "The only family I had was my mother. She died two years ago."

"Oh. I'm sorry."

"Don't be. She'd been bedridden for some time. She was in a great deal of pain. She looked forward to the release."

"It must have been difficult for you to go through."

"Yes."

He leaned against the back of the couch. "So you were an only child. I was the middle of three boys. We're each five years apart, so we didn't grow up particularly close. But for all of that, we've managed to get along fairly well through the years."

She didn't say anything, and Cameron again felt himself getting edgy. Damn, didn't the woman make any conversation other than polite brief answers to his questions?

"Would you like something to drink?" he asked. "We have a fully stocked bar, some fairly good wine, whatever you'd like."

"A glass of wine would be nice."

"Great. Give me an idea of the kind you like, and I'll see if I can find something to your taste."

She suggested a dry white wine, and he went off to get some, wondering if he should change his mind and ask Pete to fly in to the rescue. The problem was he wasn't certain who needed rescuing, himself or his very reluctant guest.

Three

———

"And then she announced to the class that she wouldn't sit next to David because boys had cooties."

Cameron began to laugh and Janine joined in. Dinner was over, and the rest of the household had long since retired. He and Janine had returned to the family room, built up the fire and continued to enjoy their wine and the relaxed conversation that had evolved imperceptibly during dinner.

"Where in the world did she get something like that?" Janine asked when she could draw breath.

"No doubt that's one of Tony's stories. I think it started when he told her that all girls have cooties. She denied it vehemently even though she didn't have the vaguest idea what he was talking about. Obviously she switched the gender to suit her own convenience."

"Tony?"

"Cole's son. He'll be eighteen this summer, but when he and Trisha get together, I swear he's no more than six!"

"Ah, yes. Trisha has spoken of him." They sat side by side on the couch, watching the flames. Never had he felt so aware of another person as he did of Janine at the moment. Letty had spoken to Allison by phone and had reassured Janine that Allison was delighted to share her clothes with her. Janine had found a tailored silk shirt and a pair of deep green slacks. Fortunately she had also been able to wear Allison's shoes, although she was barefoot at the moment. Her feet now rested next to his stockinged feet on the coffee table.

"It's late. I really should get to bed," she murmured.

"Why? You've got all day tomorrow to sleep."

"Well, actually, I promised Trisha I would color with her in the morning."

"She'll forgive you if you're a little late."

Janine rolled her head lazily to the side so that she could see him. "I've really enjoyed this evening, Cam. You've made me feel like a welcomed guest instead of a gate crasher."

"You're not a gate crasher. Not by any means. I thought I made that clear earlier. I'm touched that you care enough about Trisha to come talk to me."

"But you were right. It's really none of my business."

"I'm glad you care, Janine. Believe me." He touched his finger to her cheek, verifying what he had already suspected. Her cheek felt like satin. She smiled and her eyelashes fluttered once, then closed. He cupped her cheek with his hand and pressed a soft kiss on her lips.

She made a sound in her throat, a light humming sound of pleasure that caused a flame to shoot through him. He shifted so that he could pull her into his arms and kiss her more deeply.

When he finally lifted his head, she whispered in a drugged voice, "I don't think this is a very good idea."

He smiled at her token protest, since she hadn't moved at all, even to open her eyes. "I disagree. I think it's a wonderful idea. I've been wanting to kiss you for hours."

She opened her eyes, the lids heavy, and peered at him. "Even when I was so prim and proper?"

He grinned. "Especially when you were so prim and proper. I had a sudden longing to see you hot and bothered."

"Really?"

"Mmm-hmm."

"You are a wicked man, Cameron Callaway."

"So I've been told."

"You've plied me with gourmet food and excellent liquor. Now all I want to do is curl up like a cat and go to sleep."

"That's *all* you want?"

Even her smile was sleepy. "I guess I'm more prim and proper than you expected, huh?"

"Don't get me wrong. I'm not complaining," he replied, helping her from the couch. After thinking about that for a moment, he said, "Well, to be completely honest, maybe I *am* complaining, but just a little. I know that if I allowed you to have your way with me tonight, you'd have absolutely no respect for me in the morning.''

She choked on her laughter. "I'm impressed that you understand the situation so clearly," she said dryly. They were starting up the stairs. She glanced around and asked, "How do you keep from getting lost in here?"

"I suppose because I've lived here all my life and I've explored every inch of the place." He paused at the top of the stairs and waited for her to join him. "Remind me to take you up to explore the attic tomorrow. If you want the real scoop on the Callaways, there are several titillating journals that would scorch your fingertips to read."

She glanced at him. "And you'd let me read them?"

"Are you planning to write an exposé about us?"

"Of course not."

"Then I don't mind your reading them."

He took her hand and smoothed it across his callused palm. She had long narrow fingers that he kept fantasizing about. "May I walk you home, Ms. Talbot, ma'am?"

"Why, I'd be delighted, Mr. Callaway, sir."

She had been given one of the guest bedrooms a couple of doors down the hall from his room. In one respect she felt safe knowing that he was nearby. In another, she didn't feel safe at all.

They stopped in front of her room and he leaned his hand against the wall beside her head. "Sleep well."

"Oh, I'll do that all right. I'm almost asleep on my feet."

He leaned down and kissed her, meaning to be casual, but the kiss got out of control. He braced his other hand on the wall, effectively caging her between his forearms. She tasted so good to him, and it had been so long since he had enjoyed being with a woman.

An alarm kept ringing in the back of his head, but he ignored it, enjoying the moment. When she slipped her arms around his neck, he allowed his body to press against her so that she knew exactly how she affected him.

When they broke apart this time, they were both obviously shaken. Her eyes glittered in the shadowed hallway as she brushed her fingertips across his lips. "Good night, Cam. I'll see you in the morning."

Before he could think of anything to say, she had slipped inside the room and closed the door. He stood there staring at the door for several moments before he forced himself to walk down the hallway to his room.

Muttering, Cameron strode into the bathroom for his third shower of the day, this time without benefit of hot water. Even after he crawled into bed, he had trouble going to sleep. What the hell was happening to him? His behavior toward his daughter's teacher was incomprehensible. She was nice enough, but he wasn't interested. Not in her, not in anyone.

So why did his pulse pick up every time his thoughts turned to how she had looked leaning against the wall—her hair mussed, her eyes half-closed, her lips softly swollen from his kisses?

What was wrong with him, anyway? He was too old to be behaving like a schoolboy with his first crush.

He punched his pillow vehemently a couple of times, flopped over onto his stomach and buried his head beneath the pillow.

Not more than a few minutes later—or so it seemed to Cameron—he felt a light touch on his shoulder. For an instant he thought it was— No, he knew better. He raised his head and discovered that the small lamp next to his bed was on. He distinctly remembered turning it off when he crawled into the sack. What in the— He rolled to his side and saw Cody standing nearby, grinning, his hands on his hips.

"How did you—? Where have you—? Damn, Cody, but you can be downright exasperating," he said as he got out of bed and grabbed his brother's shoulders. "Man, you're a sight for sore eyes."

Cody chuckled. "It's good to see you, too, Cam." He paused, flicking his gaze over Cameron's nude body and added, "All of you."

Cameron shook his head, still groggy from sleep, and, covering himself with a sheet, sat down on the side of the bed. He reached for a cigarette and said, "You could call once in a while, you know, just to let somebody know you're okay."

"I'm here now, aren't I? Isn't that good enough for you?"

"How the hell did you get here? Nobody's been able to get in or out."

Cody sank into a chair near the bed. "Why not?"

"The bridge nearest the house is out. How could you not know that?"

"Because I didn't come by road."

Cameron straightened and looked at his younger brother. "You came across the Rio Grande?"

"Yep. Borrowed a friend's horse and rode over to check on things."

"What are you doing over there?"

"Minding my own business."

Cameron sighed in disgust and lit a cigarette. Then he took a long drag.

"Tell me about the bridge," Cody asked after a prolonged silence.

"Nothing much to tell. This damned rain has stirred up all kinds of trouble. Alejandro and his men have been building a modern-day ark in the barn for more than a week, convinced we're all going to need it."

"Did you get yourself a new car?" Cody asked.

"No, why?"

"I saw a little white car sitting out there with the other ranch vehicles. At least I think it was white at one time."

"Belongs to Janine."

Cody settled back in his chair with a grin. "Janine, huh? Tell me more."

"There's nothing to tell. She's Trisha's teacher and she—"

"I didn't know Trisha was in school."

"Dammit, Cody, do you want an answer or do you want to interrupt me?"

"You mean I can't do both?"

Cameron finished his cigarette and crawled back under the covers. When he reached for the light, Cody said, "All right, all right. Damn, you're a grouch, Cam. So tell me what Trisha's teacher is doing here."

Cameron plumped up his pillow, then placed his hands behind his head. "She came out to see me to talk about Trisha, and before she could leave the bridge was washed away."

"So what does she look like?"

"I didn't notice."

"Hmm. Either you're lying to me or you're in even worse shape than I thought." Cody got to his feet. "Either way, maybe I'd better talk to Cole about this latest information I've managed to dig up."

Cameron propped himself up on his elbows. "Cut the clowning, Cody. What have you found out?"

"Just what we suspected. The fire in the cotton warehouse was without doubt arson, the broken drilling equipment on the offshore rig was no accident, the lost shipment to Chicago was claimed with forged papers in St. Louis, the—"

"Swell. Just what I needed to hear."

"I tried to contact you at your office all week. All that sweet talkin' secretary of yours would tell me was that you were in court."

"I was."

"All week?"

"For the past three weeks. As far as I'm concerned I've proved that the series of so-called unrelated incidents in Corpus Christi were part of a plan to have us miss our deadlines, ruin our ability to fulfill orders, and that we are somehow being set up to lose the company."

"And what does your opposition have to say?"

"What they've said all along—prove that it was us."

"And have you?"

"At this point I just don't know. Everything's so damned circumstantial."

"What an interesting time for you to receive a visit from somebody who says she's Trisha's teacher."

"She is. I mean, Trisha recognized her."

"Of course. My point is, how did it come about that Trisha is in school in the first place? She isn't due to start until the fall."

"Yeah, I know. I had a little talk with Letty about that. It seems that when Trisha was tested she showed a lack of certain social skills, and the school felt she needed some extra time with children her own age. Letty said she didn't want me worrying about it, so she went ahead and enrolled Trisha in a semester of preschool, then told her to wait to tell me until I came home as a surprise." He thought about the confrontation between him and Janine. Some surprise. "The biggest surprise was that Trisha could keep a secret that long. She hasn't been very happy with school, from what I can gather."

"Interesting."

"But not surprising. I didn't like school, either, at first."

"No, I mean that Trisha's teacher developed such an interest in her new student that she came out to discuss her with you, just at this time."

"You think there's some connection?"

"It isn't paranoia when someone really is out to get you, bro. We've got an overwhelming amount of evidence to show that somebody, somewhere, has a real hatred for the Callaways."

"I don't think it's Janine," he mumbled, thinking about the evening he'd just spent with her.

"Probably not, but I'm far from convinced that she isn't being used by someone to get more information about us. Isn't it convenient that she's now stranded here with you, so that she has full access to the entire house?"

Cameron groaned. "And I just offered to let her read some of the diaries and journals upstairs that would tell her even more."

"How did she respond?"

"Well, she didn't say no. She acted a little surprised that I offered."

"I'm more than a little surprised. I'm flabbergasted. You're the most private one of our whole bunch."

Cameron grinned. "And you're the most suspicious."

"What did you say she looked like?"

"I didn't."

"Maybe you'd better. I may have seen her, or at least heard about her."

"I doubt it. She's only lived here a year. She's from Colorado. I'd guess she's somewhere between her late twenties or possibly early thirties. She's about the same size as Allison, so she's wearing her clothes. She's got long reddish-brown hair, I guess you'd call it auburn, and green eyes. She's slender but well proportioned."

"For somebody who didn't notice what she looks like, you did a damn fine job of describing her. I was planning to leave tonight, but I may stick around tomorrow to get acquainted."

Cameron had a sudden urge to tell his brother to leave her alone, but stopped himself. What difference would it make to him if Cody met Janine? Maybe they would hit it off. Did he care?

For some reason he couldn't fathom, he *did* care. He shut his eyes for a moment, wishing he had a better understanding of some of his actions over the past several hours.

"Sorry I woke you," Cody said, coming to his feet. "I think I'll go on to bed. I'd hoped to get in and out of here without Letty knowing about it, but I suppose I can listen to her scolding with good grace. I should be used to it by now."

"Letty's not so bad. I'm sure it wasn't the greatest moment in her life to have her brother and his wife killed, leaving her three boys to look after."

"Two. Cole was already twenty. So that left all her time to concentrate on you at fifteen and me at ten."

"She never could find you."

Cody flashed the grin that always caused everyone to forgive him, no matter what he had done. "Yeah, but she certainly did everything in her power to keep me hemmed in when she did."

"Is that why you've refused to help Cole and me with the businesses?"

"Partly. My mind doesn't run to figures and strategy."

"Just to disappearing and partying?"

"Something like that."

Cameron shook his head. "Cole and I worry about you, you know."

"What a waste of energy. I can take care of myself." He opened the door and glanced over his shoulder. "Your little schoolteacher isn't sleeping in my bed, is she?" he asked with a wolfish gleam in his eye.

"She's not even in your wing. Go to bed and try to stay out of trouble, if that's possible."

Cody gave him a two-finger salute, a parody of a parade-ground sign of respect, and closed the door behind him.

Cameron shook his head wearily, then leaned over and turned off the lamp beside the bed. He continued to lie there, staring up at the shadowy ceiling.

Could it be possible that Janine was somehow connected to the events of the past few years? The Callaway brothers had finally faced the fact that someone behind the scenes was working hard to discredit them wherever possible, to inflict as much property damage as possible, and was probably responsible for the deaths of their parents and Cameron's wife.

He wasn't certain where Cody found his sources, but they had become invaluable in tracing people and events. Perhaps Cody was using his playboy image to cover the investigative work he had been doing for the family for the past few years. Then again, he might be using the investigation to cover his urge to be free to roam as he pleased, to refuse to have anything to do with the family business, and to pop in and out of their lives at will.

Cameron would be interested to see what Cody thought of Janine. For the first time in a long while, he no longer trusted his own judgment. Sometime during that last kiss they had shared he had lost his objectivity about the woman who showed so much concern for his daughter.

Janine awoke the next morning with a raging headache. She had no one but herself to blame. She knew better than to have more than one glass of wine, but she had ignored her usual good sense. She found

Cameron Callaway captivating, and she had wanted to stay in his company for as long as possible the night before. She had spent the evening looking for ways to bring a smile to his face. She had rejoiced in his laughter, intuitively knowing that he found few things in his life amusing.

She felt his suffering and wished for some knowledge of how to relieve it. Their evening in front of the fireplace, watching the dancing flames, had been magical, as though time had been suspended while they learned more about each other.

She had told him a little more about her childhood, about growing up without a father, about spending her free time after school looking after the younger children who lived in her neighborhood.

He had told her what life had been like for him, growing up on a ranch in south Texas, knowing that he was observed and reported on because he was a Callaway. According to him, he had been the quiet one, the one who entertained himself by reading and studying, the one who hated the spotlight that shone on him.

Cameron had become very real to Janine during those few hours together. Very real, and for the first time since she met him, she had recognized his vulnerability.

Janine forced herself out of bed and into the shower, praying that she had something in her purse to help her aching head. By the time she was ready to go downstairs, the aspirin she had taken had eased her pain somewhat, and she vowed not to make a similar mistake in the near future.

As soon as she walked into the large dining room, a man she had never seen before came toward her, his hand extended. "You must be Trisha's teacher. I had no idea teachers came in such delectable packages these days."

He was tall, with golden-blond hair and audacious eyes, but it was the outrageous grin that told her his teasing was all in good fun and not to be taken seriously. She took his hand and shook it gravely.

"Janine Talbot," she said in her most prim tone.

He immediately ducked his chin and said in a mock-shy voice, "Cody Callaway, at your service, ma'am." He kept her hand and led her to the place next to him at the table.

"Cody," she repeated. "You're the youngest of the three, aren't you?"

He peered both ways before leaning forward and saying, "Just a nasty rumor the other two started about me, you know. I let them get away with it, of course. Gives them such a sense of superiority."

He really was incorrigible. She began to laugh. He nodded as though pleased with her reaction to his teasing, and poured her a cup of coffee.

"Have you seen Trisha this morning?" she asked.

"Nope. I haven't been downstairs all that long, myself. Had a rather late night."

Janine caught herself rubbing her forehead in an effort to ease the ache. "I know what you mean," she said ruefully. "I'm afraid I don't have much of a head for wine."

"Aha! Everything is coming clear to me now, my pretty. My dastardly brother took advantage of your weakness, did he, and plied you with spirits in order to have his evil way with you." He paused, and she knew he saw the blush that covered her cheeks, blast it. In a nonchalant tone, he added, "Cam's smarter than I gave him credit for," and took a sip of coffee, his eyes filled with amusement.

"Of course he didn't take advantage of me," she said in an attempt to explain her betraying color. "He was very much a gentleman."

"Are we talking about my brother? The guy that's about my height, with brown hair and—"

"Oh, you. Are you ever serious?"

He clasped her hand between his two and peered soulfully into her eyes. "I would be quite willing to show you my serious side," he said, his voice sultry. "If you wish."

"All right, Cody." Janine heard Cam's voice behind her and turned to see him coming toward them, a frown on his face. "Do you have to hit on every female you meet? Give it a rest, will you? At least let her have her first cup of coffee."

Janine tugged her hand away from Cody's grasp, knowing that she was turning every shade of red. Cameron would think that the two of them had been flirting when, in fact, they had been making fun of the idea. Surely he didn't think she was the type of woman who would be sharing kisses with him in the evening and making up to his brother the next morning?

From the aloof stare he gave her as he sat directly across the table from her, that was exactly what he was thinking. Either that, or he didn't care what she did or with whom.

Well, she wasn't about to explain to him. She owed him nothing, regardless of the previous night's events.

"Did you notice the sunshine today, bro?" Cody asked.

"No."

"Didn't think so. Maybe this means there's going to be a change in the weather pattern. I know how you're itching to get back to work. I bet you can hardly wait to—"

"Cody, would you chill out for a while—please? I didn't have the best of nights, and I would really appreciate being able to enjoy my morning coffee in peace and quiet."

"Oh, sure, no problem. You and Janine seem to have suffered similar ailments." He glanced at Janine. "Would you like some aspirin?"

She shook her head. "I've already taken some, thanks. I'll be all right." She kept her eyes on her coffee.

Cameron looked at the two of them seated side by side. "I don't guess I need to introduce the two of you. You seem to have struck up quite a friendship already."

Cody beamed. "So we did. It must have been kismet, or maybe—"

"Cody," Cameron growled warningly.

His brother gave him a sparkling smile and picked up his cup of coffee.

Janine watched the brothers, wondering whether or not they got along. There was a strong family resemblance, but their personalities were very different. Janine had always wanted a brother. Cody was exactly what she had imagined a brother would be. She had immediately felt relaxed and at ease with him.

Her feelings toward Cameron were considerably different.

Rosie brought platters of eggs, bacon, biscuits and gravy out and set them all on the table. The three of them ate in silence except for brief requests to pass the butter, or salt and pepper, or for more coffee.

By the time they finished, Janine felt uncomfortable with the silence, but she had no intention of being the one to break it. All she knew was that she didn't want Cameron to be angry with her. She wasn't certain why, exactly. She just knew that was the way she felt.

The swinging door from the kitchen opened, and Janine looked up, thankful for the interruption, thinking that Rosie had come to pick up their dishes. Instead, a middle-aged man in worn jeans and shirt, wearing boots and carrying a hat, stood there.

"Sorry to bother you at breakfast, Cameron," he began.

"No bother, Alejandro. We're just enjoying last cups of coffee. How about joining us?"

"No, thanks. Thought I'd let you know that me and the boys think we can start on some kind of temporary bridge today, but I wanted to check with you first."

Both Cameron and Cody pushed back their chairs and stood. Cameron looked at Janine. "If you'll excuse us, we'll see what we can do to help you leave as soon as possible."

Cody began to laugh. "Why, Cam, you sound downright inhospitable. Here's your hat and coat, ma'am. Don't let the door hit you on the way out." He winked at Janine. "He just never did get his social graces down pat like he should have." He took her hand and raised it to his lips. "Sorry to have to leave you, pretty lady. We'll be back as soon as we can."

She kept her eyes averted, not wanting to see Cameron's reaction to his brother's clowning.

The three men left the room through the kitchen doorway, which presumably led them to a back exit. Janine felt a great deal of relief at having the chance to be alone for a while. She finished her coffee and stood.

She would go find Trisha in an effort to recreate the comfortable existence with which she was familiar—being around children.

Four

———

Alejandro headed toward one of the pickup trucks and Cameron and Cody followed him. Cameron knew that Alejandro was being polite in seeking advice. He ran the ranch in its entirety, carrying full responsibility for what took place on the premises. Letty was in charge of the Big House and the employees who worked inside, but Alejandro had the final word on everything else. However, in all the time Cameron had known him, Alejandro would always consult whatever brother happened to be in residence at the time. The fact that, in the end, each of them went along with his suggestions never changed his way of handling things.

Alejandro got behind the wheel. The other two slid into the front seat of the pickup from the other side.

"What the hell was that all about?" Cameron growled once Cody slammed the door behind them and Alejandro drove out of the parking area.

Cody gave him an innocent smile. "What are you talking about?"

"Why were you coming on to Janine?"

Cody lifted his brow. "Was I?"

"Is it some kind of game with you, to flirt with every woman you meet?"

"If it is, what does it matter to you?"

Normally Cameron had no reaction to what other people chose to do. So why was he so upset now?

He had to face his own feelings and stop running from them. He was attracted to the woman, no doubt about that. So what was he going to do about it?

He had been alone for four years now—not that he was considering matrimony. He wanted none of that, no reminders of a past that still carried too much pain for him. But what was wrong with an intimate friendship? They were both adults, weren't they?

"It matters in this case. So how about slacking off with this one and giving me some space," he finally muttered.

Cody gave him a sharp look. "I thought you weren't interested."

Cameron knew he looked as sheepish as he felt. "So did I. Guess I was wrong, huh?"

Cody laughed and Cameron found himself joining in.

"Good for you, Cam. It's just what you need."

"Nothing serious, you understand." He felt it imperative that Cody not read more into this than he intended.

"Sure. Who better than me can understand that kind of relationship?"

For some reason, that didn't make Cameron feel much better about what he was considering. Both he and Cole had always been troubled by Cody's lifestyle. Was he now actually considering imitating it?

He had never played the adult dating game. He and Andrea had met in college, had dated for three years and had gotten married the month after graduation. Their lives had flowed smoothly. She had become a buyer for one of the stores in San Antonio and had enjoyed traveling until they decided to start their family. He had planned his work in order to travel with her. They had had a wonderful time together. They had enjoyed doing the same kinds of things. Once Andrea was gone, he had buried himself in his work. Any spare time he had was spent with Trisha.

Now he was looking to change all of that by the simple task of asking Janine Talbot for a date. With a sinking feeling in his stomach, he realized that he didn't know how to go about it.

He wasn't at all sure he was ready for this next step. Having met her, he also realized that he didn't want to let her slip out of his life.

"I like butterflies best," Trisha said, a small furrow between her brows as she concentrated on her picture.

Janine looked at the picture and smiled. This was going to be one of the brightest butterflies nature could have possibly created. Trisha had used every color she could find in the shoe box where her crayons were kept.

"What do you like about butterflies?"

"They is so pretty, and they fly around and do things, and . . ." She paused, thinking, then shrugged. "You know. I bet it would be fun being a butterfly, don't you?"

Janine grinned. "Only if you don't get airsick!"

"What's that?"

"When you're flying around and your stomach acts like it's still on the ground."

Trisha studied her teacher. "Did that ever happen to you?"

Janine nodded. "Once, when I was flying and the plane was trying to get around a storm. My stomach much preferred staying on the ground that day."

Trisha grinned. "Was you scared?"

"Maybe a little."

"What do you like best?" the girl said, gazing down at her butterfly.

Janine thought for a moment. "I think that, of everything I like, rainbows are my favorite. They seem magical to me somehow. I'm always excited whenever I see one."

"Me, too. Maybe we can look for rainbows together some day."

"Maybe."

"What interesting thing have you two been up to?"

Janine whirled around and looked toward the doorway of the family room. Cameron strode in, a grin on his face. His earlier somber mood had obviously left. Either that, or he had recently received some very good news.

"Were they able to make a temporary bridge?" she asked as Trisha scrambled from her chair and went racing to her father.

"Daddy! Come look and see what me and Missy Talbot colored." He leaned down and picked up his bouncing daughter and carried her over to the coffee table, where Janine sat and where their creative efforts were displayed. "See? Hers are panda bears. Aren't they cute? Mine's a butterfly."

"Two artists obviously hard at work," he said solemnly, studying each piece as though considering the purchase of major art. Janine enjoyed watching Trisha puff up with pride as he made first one comment, then another, about the various efforts. He seemed to know exactly what to say without a hint of self-consciousness.

Then he glanced up and caught her watching him. His gaze seemed to pin her where she sat. "I'm afraid there's not much hope of our getting out of here for at least two, possibly three more days. The runoff is still too swift to chance working in the water, and the creek continues to be at flood level."

He sounded remarkably cheerful for a man marooned.

"I don't know what to do," Janine replied, expressing her worry out loud. "I'm expected to be at work at eight in the morning."

"You'll have to call and explain the situation. With the flooding in surrounding areas, there's a good chance there'll be no school."

She eyed him uncertainly. He appeared almost pleased.

"Isn't this going to pose a problem for you?" she asked.

"Not really. As soon as my secretary arrives at work in the morning, I'll give her a call and have her fax the most urgent business to me." He leaned back so that he was sitting next to Janine, their shoulders almost touching. Meanwhile, Trisha had scooted off his lap and was now attacking a brand-new picture with renewed fervor.

Janine had trouble meeting his gaze. He seemed to be amused by something.

"Well," she said uncertainly, "I suppose we'll have to make the best of the situation."

His smile broadened. "My sentiments, exactly. We'll use the time to get better acquainted."

Janine thought of his words later while she dressed for dinner. Cameron had spent the rest of the day with her and Trisha, entertaining them, asking questions. He had continued to draw her out until she realized with something of a start that she had told him almost her whole life story.

At one point she commented on the fact that she hadn't seen Cody since breakfast. She had been startled by his smile, which could have been one of satisfaction, when Cameron casually explained that Cody had left. Cody had chosen an unorthodox way to get there, and she assumed he had left on horseback, as well.

She had liked Cody and was comfortable around him. She felt anything but comfortable around Cameron, who was waiting for her to join him downstairs.

Now she gazed into the mirror, struck by the bold colors of the gown she wore. The shimmering emerald green of the cloth made her hair look redder and her eyes seem greener.

Cameron had told her a little about his artistic sister-in-law. She and his brother Cole had grown up on the ranch together. Janine wondered what it would be like to have had someone in her life besides her mother. She almost envied Cole and Allison their closeness.

She attempted to twist her hair into a coil, but it seemed to have developed a will of its own, defying her every effort to subdue it. Tossing her head in frustration, she grabbed her brush and once again allowed her hair to fall to her shoulders. As a result, the combination of the hairdo and the bright hue of the beautiful gown made her feel, when she stared into the mirror, as though she were looking at a stranger.

With a defiant toss of her head, she decided that for the next few days she would allow herself to play a new role, one that allowed her to flirt gently with a very attractive man. He had made no effort all day to hide his interest in her. She could only conclude that his earlier gruff demeanor at breakfast meant that he didn't happen to be a morning person.

As soon as she started down the stairway, Cameron appeared at the bottom. The look he gave her was so heated it caused her temperature to rise. She stood firm with her new resolve and met his gaze with a smile.

"I have a surprise for you," he said, reaching for her hand and pulling her close when she stood beside him.

"That's nothing new," she said with a grin. "You're full of them."

He looked pleased. "You think so?"

"Without a doubt." She glanced around. "Where's Trisha?"

"That's part of the surprise." He led her toward the back of the house, then through a couple of rooms to the solarium, where she and Trisha had been the day before. If she had thought it a magical room then, it was even more so now in the soft moonlight that came through the glassed ceiling. A table for two was set next to one of the glassed walls, with candles illuminating the surrounding area. A candelabra filled with candles sat among the greenery and the candlelight was reflected in the many panes of glass surrounding them. "Oh, Cam. This is beautiful."

"I sat with Trisha while she had her supper, oversaw her bath, tucked her into bed, read her two stories and left her sound asleep, just so you and I could have some time together."

"But what about your aunt?"

"Actually, I got the idea for this when she told me she was tired and decided to have a small tray in her room. She'll probably watch television until all hours, but at least she'll be resting."

"Is she feeling okay?"

"She insists she's fine. She becomes infuriated if any of us dares to suggest that her age might hold her back some. She made it clear that she was able to rest now that I was home to look after Trisha." He seated her at the table and then sat across from her. "Of course she's right. Between the two of you this weekend, I've definitely been made aware of my short-comings as a parent.''

Janine suddenly felt very small. She made herself hold eye contact with him. ''It was very presumptu-ous of me to think I knew what was best for your daughter.''

''The point was well taken, though—once I calmed down and thought about it. I'm thinking about tak-ing Trisha to San Antonio so that she'll be with me there. However, I'm going to have to find a live-in housekeeper, check out the schools and see how she feels about relocating, beforehand. Although we lived in San Antonio her first year, she doesn't remember it. This has always been home for her. I made that my excuse for leaving her here for so long, but what I've come to understand is that home for her will be any-where I am.''

Janine felt a pang somewhere in the region of her heart. She had grown to love Trisha in the few weeks the girl had been in her class. ''I know she'll want to be with you. There's not a doubt in my mind, after all of my conversations with her.''

''I think that's what really got me to looking at our situation. If she discusses her feelings with someone she barely knows, she must be more disturbed by my absences than I had guessed.''

''If you need to hear it from me, I think you're do-ing the right thing, even though I'm going to miss her very much.''

He leaned over and took her hand. ''Well, maybe we can do something to alleviate that somewhat.'' He gave her hand a gentle squeeze and picked up the bottle that had been resting in a small bucket of ice. "How about a glass of wine?"

Wasn't he going to explain his enigmatic remark? Apparently not, as he waited for her to respond to his question.

"One glass. I'm definitely making that my limit."

He smiled. "Never let it be said that I lured you past any of your limits."

Rosie came in, carrying a tray. She placed salads in front of them and left with a small smile hovering on her lips.

"Thank you for thinking of this. I can't believe how beautiful everything is." She looked toward the fountain and discovered that the water was flowing for the first time since she had arrived. Its musical trickle could be heard in a muted subtle way she found captivating.

She was hardly aware of what they had for dinner. All she knew was that Rosie unobtrusively served them while they talked. They seemed to have so much to discover about each other. They talked about the most recent books they had read, their favorite pastimes, their hobbies, and both discovered that they were often content to be alone. Most of their enjoyment came from solitary entertainment.

"I know this is impertinent of me, but I really want to know," Cameron began when they were having coffee.

She smiled. "Ask away."

"I can't understand why you're single. It has to be through choice. Or am I erroneously presuming that you've never been married?"

Her bubble burst with his words and she came tumbling back into reality. Not that she blamed him for his curiosity. On his own accord he had told her about Andrea—how they had met, their life together and the devastation of her death. She knew that by opening up to her he had assumed that she would be willing to do the same.

She searched for something to say, something that would explain without touching the core of her pain.

"I, uh, never had any desire to marry, I guess. Or met anyone with whom I thought I could be happy. As I said earlier, I'm really a very solitary person and quite content with my own company."

"But you're so wonderful with children. I would expect you to want a houseful of your own."

She dropped her hands to her lap so that he could not see the tension as she gripped them. "That's why I chose my particular vocation. I enjoy children. I just don't want them around all the time. I need my solitude. This way I have the best of both worlds."

His gaze never left her face. She wished she could tell what he was thinking, but she couldn't. Not that it mattered, of course, what he thought.

"Well—" she began to push her chair backward "—I think I'll—"

He came to his feet. "I hope you aren't too tired for at least a dance or two."

That stopped her. "Dance?" she asked, hearing her voice squeak with surprise.

Cameron walked over to the wall and flipped a switch. Soft music filled the room. When he came toward her, he looked amused. "I'd intended to turn that on earlier, but I forgot. It's wired to play in every room, but we seldom use it." He held out his arms to her. "Shall we?"

How could she resist? She moved into his arms and felt as though she belonged there. The music was evocative of another era, the smoky sounds of a saxophone nudging something deep inside her to awaken.

She rested her head against his shoulder, allowing him to draw her closer until both of his arms were around her and her arms were around his neck. She could smell the freshly laundered scent of his shirt, mingled with the spicy after-shave he wore. Never before had a man had such an effect on her.

He explored the length of her spine with a light touch that nevertheless seemed to leave his imprint tingling along her back.

By the time he lifted her chin with his forefinger, she knew she was rapidly losing control of her reactions to him. For that brief moment in time, she didn't care.

He brushed his lips lazily across her mouth in a gentle teasing motion, causing her to want more. She wanted him to kiss her the way he had the night before when they had stood outside her bedroom door. For that fleeting instant she had allowed herself the luxury of feeling everything she was experiencing, without her mind controlling her emotions and shutting them down. Like a potential drug addict with her first rush of pleasure, she was hungry for a similar experience. She tightened her arms and he seemed to understand, for when he claimed her lips, she felt seared with his heat.

Because of the tight rein she had always kept on her emotions, she had had no idea what it would feel like to experience passion—until now. Like a sudden flame, her newly awakened desire swept over her, engulfing her, leaving her trembling in its wake.

Cameron seemed to sense her abandonment to the moment. With a groan that she felt echo deep within her, he picked her up and carried her to the rattan sofa nearby. Sitting with her draped across him, he continued to kiss her.

When he slid his hand over one of her breasts she tensed. His fingers moved tenderly across the tip, teasing and tantalizing. Instead of drawing away, she surprised herself by pressing closer to him.

When he finally lifted his head, Cameron said, "Lordy, woman, but you go to my head."

Her laugh, when it came, was shaky.

He hugged her, his touch soothing now as he stroked her back. "I owe you an apology. I know you're going to find this hard to believe, but this really isn't a seduction scene."

She leaned back to look at his face. Even with the shadows in the room, she could see he was flushed.

"What is it?" she asked, unable to resist.

He glanced around the room, at the cozy table for two with the tall taper candles still gleaming, then at the other candles placed about the room.

"Would you believe romantic?"

"It's certainly that," she agreed.

He leaned his head against the back of the sofa, shut his eyes and sighed. "I feel like a fool."

"Why?"

He opened his eyes and looked at her with a hint of a smile at the corners of his mouth. "I don't know anything about dating. I guess maybe I've watched too much television. I just thought maybe I'd set a mood and see what happened. I didn't mean to get carried away."

"You weren't alone. As I recall, you had my full cooperation."

He raised his head, his smile growing. "Hey, that's right."

"You certainly didn't force me or take advantage of me."

He slipped his hand, which he'd moved to her waist, back to her breast. "No?" His eyes gleamed with mischief in the candlelight.

She lifted his hand and slid her fingers between his. "No," she replied with a smile. "However, we don't want to start something we have no intention of finishing."

"We don't?"

He looked so crestfallen she almost laughed. She was ninety percent certain he was teasing her, but that ten percent doubt made her careful of hurting his feelings.

"No," she said gently. "We don't."

Once again he closed his eyes and leaned his head back. "Darn."

She began to laugh and he joined her. When the laughter faded she realized that he was staring at her intently. When he kissed her this time, there was a difference, a new tenderness that touched her heart. Each time she felt his lips lessening the pressure against her mouth to draw away, she felt a sense of regret. He must have felt the same way, because he never quite released her lips. Instead, he increased the pressure once more.

Finally she realized that she was losing control again. She hid her head in his shoulder.

"What's wrong? I've kept my hands to myself."

They were still holding hands.

"This is dangerous."

"You think so?"

"I know so."

"But it's fun," he offered hopefully.

"Yes, I'll certainly admit that."

"And I think we're both enjoying it."

She loved this light side of him, a side she hadn't seen before this evening. She wondered how often he allowed himself to unbend and tease in this way.

"Cameron?"

"Hmm?"

"Neither of us is the type to lose our heads and hearts in passion."

"We're not?"

"Uh-uh."

"You're sure?"

"Uh-huh."

"So what do you suggest we do?"

"Go to bed."

"Hell of an idea! Let's—"

"No, no, no," she said with a chuckle. "It's time for each of us to retire to our respective bedrooms where we will then go to bed and get some sleep."

The look he gave her was no longer teasing, but filled with heat. "Do you honestly believe that last part?"

She sighed. "Perhaps not completely. But it's for the best."

"Why?"

She looked down at their clasped hands. "Because I'm not the kind of person who has casual affairs."

"Neither am I."

This time she had no doubt in her mind that he was serious. The intensity of his look caused her to tremble. She briefly closed her eyes, then forced herself to meet his gaze. "I don't date much, either."

"Neither do I," he repeated, "but I'd like to change that."

"I suppose the point I'm trying to make is that I don't want to change it." After the way she had been behaving, she could understand his skeptical expression. She felt the heat in her cheeks and knew she was blushing. "There's no future in it," she attempted to explain.

"Does there have to be a future?"

"Well, most people expect a relationship to go somewhere."

"Well, I'm not ready for a relationship that's going to 'go somewhere.' But I would like to get to know you better, and I've been encouraged to think you might feel the same way."

She could feel her heart racing. "Is that all?" she finally asked.

He cocked his head and grinned. "Well, I don't have a master plan mapped out just yet to submit for your approval, but give me a few days and maybe I can come up with something."

When she didn't respond he went on. "I'm not talking about something serious here, you know. There are times when I receive invitations where I'm expected to bring a guest. There are times when maybe I'd like to have a little company. There are even times when I'd like to pick up the phone and chat with someone. Do you see anything wrong in our forming a friendship that might include those activities?''

In all honesty she couldn't. She shook her head.

"Good enough," he said, standing up but still holding her as her feet came to the floor. "Then we know where we stand, don't we?"

"I, uh, suppose so."

"I'll try not to monopolize your time, but it would be nice to know I could call you once in a while."

She gazed into his shadowed face. "I'd like that."

"So would I," he murmured, before kissing her good-night.

Five

Cameron came awake with a start, blinking in an attempt to clear his vision. Early-morning sunlight poured through the window. He groaned. How the hell could it be morning when he didn't feel as though he had slept all night?

His dreams had kept him restless and wakeful for the past three nights. He was no longer dreaming about the crash. Now the only subject his subconscious dwelled on was Janine. Janine in bed with him, reaching for him, wanting him... Janine who left him aching and feverish, enticing him even in his sleep....

Damn. He sat up and rested his elbows on his knees. For the past two days he had not touched her. He had learned a valuable lesson after that first night of heated dreams. He had seen no reason to continue torturing himself by kissing her again. Unfortunately his new decision in no way lessened his awareness of her whenever he saw her.

Letty had made herself scarce since Janine had arrived, leaving Cameron and Trisha to entertain her. Trisha had certainly done her part. She made it clear that she was delighted to have Missy Talbot all to herself.

Cameron had worked in the study, going through papers, giving dictation over the phone to his secretary, until the sounds of laughter often impinged on his concentration and he would wander into the other room to see what was so funny.

Later he would become aware that he had ended up playing games with them and leaving his work unattended.

Cameron couldn't remember a time in his life when he had been quite so distracted in such a positive way.

He smiled to himself, thinking about the sound of Trisha's uninhibited laughter. He had never before heard such a spontaneously joyful sound coming from his daughter. He had been touched, even while he felt guilty, realizing how little he had done to add to her enjoyment of life.

Letty had been right. Trisha *had* needed to be around other people. Typically Letty had gone ahead and done what she felt was best without bothering to check with him. What he had to face was that, as long as he left Trisha with Letty, she would be the person in charge.

Was that what he wanted? Was that what Andrea would have wanted?

Andrea. This was the first time she had come into his mind unaccompanied by pain and a sense of loss.

How strange. He had grown accustomed to thinking of her in those terms. Now he could see her more clearly. He knew with a certainty that Andrea would not have tolerated her daughter's isolation. She would have done something to prevent it long before now.

Cameron knew he would have to do something about it, too, and soon. He had some ideas but wasn't certain how to go about implementing them. He threw back the covers and strode toward the bathroom and shower. He would discuss the matter with Janine.

Janine was already at the table sipping coffee when he appeared.

"You're up bright and early today," he said with a grin, taking a seat across from her.

"I'm used to getting up early, I suppose. Plus, I'm feeling so guilty not being there to help with classes."

"You're sure they've opened the schools again?"

"Yes. I listened for school announcements this morning on the radio. Everything's returning to normal. Three days of sunshine has helped tremendously."

Rosie brought in their breakfast and for several moments there was little conversation. Once he was finished, Cameron poured them another cup of coffee and said, "Then there's a good chance we'll be able to cross the creek today."

He watched her eyes light up and recognized his own dismay that she was so eager to get away. "Why, that's wonderful. I'm sure you'll be pleased to be back at work."

Normally he would be, so he nodded without committing perjury by verbally agreeing with her.

"Janine, I need your help."

She picked up her coffee and held the cup with both hands. "Oh?" she asked, and he could not only hear but see her wariness.

"About Trisha."

Her smile of relief was almost comical. "Why, certainly, Cam."

"I've been giving serious consideration to what we discussed about her. I know it will be a major adjustment for her, but I'm definitely considering moving her to San Antonio to be with me."

"I think she'd love that. I really do."

"The thing is, I'll need someone to look after her."

"That goes without saying. I'm certain that if you check with the employment services they'll find someone qualified to stay with her when you're not there."

"I was wondering if you would consider being the one. I mean, Trisha already knows and trusts you, and I..." He paused when he saw the shocked look on her face.

"I can't do that," she finally said. "I'm sorry. I would like to help you as much as possible, but that just wouldn't work. I mean, I have a contract at the school, and I can't just walk away from it. They're depending on me. And besides..."

He waited, and when she just shook her head he repeated. "Besides?"

She dropped her gaze to her coffee. "I don't think it would be a very good idea for the two of us to live in the same place."

"Oh?" He was more than a little interested to hear her elaborate on that one!

"I mean, Trisha is used to having a more mature woman, like your aunt, looking after her. I doubt she would accept me."

"But she already has."

"As her teacher, yes. For a few short hours in the day when she sees all the other children obeying me. But I don't think she'd respond in the same way on a daily basis."

"You've gotten along with her during this visit."

"Of course. We both understand the rules. I am the guest. She is playing hostess and has been very diligent in entertaining me. Knowing my role, I have been most careful not to correct her in any way, or to suggest how she conduct herself or what schedule to keep. Your aunt has continued to be in charge."

Cameron felt frustrated. All her arguments were rational and logical, but they had nothing to do with the real issue. "Andrea was about the same age as you. Trisha would have been raised by a young woman had her mother lived."

"Yes, I understand that. But the fact is that Andrea isn't here and Trisha's not used to someone my age taking charge of her."

"So you're saying no?"

"That's correct."

"Damn." He stared at her, wishing he could think of something to say to change her mind.

"However..."

"Yes?"

"I could still come to San Antonio and visit with Trisha so that she won't feel cut off completely. Perhaps my school could recommend a preschool near your home. I'll ask."

"You'd do that?"

"Certainly."

"Would you consider coming to visit me, as well?" She eyed him a little uncertainly.

"I mean, just as a friend, of course. Nothing serious. I've enjoyed getting to know you. I'd miss seeing you."

She smiled. "I'd like that."

He held out his hand across the table and she willingly placed hers in it. "Thank you," he said, feeling as though the jury had just come in with a favorable verdict on a case he hadn't been at all certain he'd had a chance of winning.

The phone rang two days later. Without glancing up from the contract he'd been looking over, he hit the intercom button. "Yes?"

His secretary's voice answered. "A Ms. Janine Talbot on line three."

Cameron felt as though he had just been zapped by a bolt of lightning. His whole body tingled at the mention of her name. "Thanks."

He reached for the phone. "Janine! It's good to hear from you. I take it you made it home all right the other day."

"Yes, thank you." She sounded very prim and proper. "I spoke with the principal of our school and she gave me the names of a few schools in your area of San Antonio. I thought you might want to look them over."

"Great idea. Hold on, let me find something to write on." His desk looked as though a tornado had come through. Piles of paper were everywhere. He pulled out a lined yellow pad from the bottom of one disordered stack, further dislodging other papers. "Ready."

She gave the names to him, along with addresses and telephone numbers. A very thorough lady. When she was finished she added, "Trisha came back to school today. She told me that her aunt had insisted she get out of the house because she was driving them all crazy. Trisha was quite proud of her accomplishment."

Cameron chuckled. "Knowing her, I'm sure she was."

"She misses you."

"Yeah. I talked to her last night. She wanted to know when I was coming back."

"And you said?"

He sighed. "I've got to stay in town over the weekend. I go back to trial on Monday, and I need to go over my summation a few more times to make sure I'm covering everything."

"I see."

"You have to understand that by the time I get there, Trisha is already in bed and I need to leave so early to get back that she's still in bed. She wouldn't even know I was there."

He didn't know why it was so important for him to make her understand. He just knew that it was.

"Cam?"

"Hmm?"

"How would you feel about my bringing her in to see you tomorrow evening for a couple of hours? We could be there when you take a break, maybe have something to eat. She could always sleep on the way home."

For a moment he was too choked up to say anything. "You'd do that for us?"

"Yes."

"I'd like that. I'd like it very much."

"Fine. Let me know where to meet you and when. You might want to let your aunt know our plans, so she won't think I'm kidnapping Trisha."

"I'll do that." He gave her the address of his condo and said, "I should be there by six-thirty, no later than seven."

"I'll let you get back to work. We'll see you tomorrow night at seven."

Cameron hung up the phone, smiling to himself. Whether Janine Talbot wanted to admit it or not, she was growing attached to the Callaways. He planned to do everything in his power to become a habit in her life.

The next afternoon, Janine stood in the middle of her bedroom floor turning slowly so that she would view the clothes laid out on the bed, over the chair, hanging on the closet door, and draped over her vanity stool and bentwood rocker.

Practically everything she owned was strewn around the room. She couldn't believe how undecided she was about what to wear on her trip to San Antonio. Glancing at her watch, she groaned. She had less than twenty minutes before she needed to leave to pick up Trisha.

Why was she being so silly about this? It wasn't as though she hadn't just spent last weekend around him.

However, the fact that she wore someone else's clothes may have given him a different impression of her. Now that she looked at her own wardrobe, she realized how drab it was. Her suits were basic tans and browns, light and navy blues and one black one. Her blouses were brighter, but not by much. The pink dress on the rocker was the most colorful thing she owned, and she wasn't at all sure it was appropriate for the occasion.

But then, what was? She was arranging transportation so that a little girl could see her daddy, that was all. Before she could finish the thought, a tiny inner voice whispered, *Oh, yeah?* She couldn't honestly respond with a firm rebuttal.

Okay. She would admit it. She had missed him. Janine had been delighted when Trisha showed up at school once again, full of mischief and vitality. In the past, she had taken special pains not to get too involved with her students and most especially not to have a favorite. However, even before she met Cameron she knew that Trisha had gotten past all her rules and defenses. She made every effort not to show favoritism, nor let Trisha get away with misbehaving.

Interestingly, Trisha was more outgoing with the children yesterday than she had ever been before. Was she feeling more secure? Janine wondered.

She grabbed the pink dress and slipped it over her head, smoothing it at her waist and hips. The soft color looked brighter with her auburn hair. One of her friends at school had coaxed her into buying it. She had no reason to wear it before, feeling that it was too light-colored for school; it would quickly get soiled there.

For the first time since she had purchased it, she was glad her friend had urged her to buy it. She looked younger somehow, more like the woman she had been at the ranch.

There was no time left to put her hair up, so she brushed it out and allowed it to hang around her shoulders. She stared into the mirror, amazed at the sparkle in her eyes. She couldn't fool herself—she was eager to see Cameron again. Her feelings for him were continuing to grow without encouragement of any kind.

By the time she reached the ranch house, or as Cameron and Cody had called it, the Big House, she was more in command of herself. As soon as she knocked, Rosie opened the door.

"Hello, Ms. Talbot. It's good to see you again."

Janine grinned. "It's good to be back. Is Letty here?"

"No, ma'am. She's visiting with friends, but Trisha is all ready to go."

Trisha had heard their voices and now she came running out of the solarium. "You're here! You're here!" she shouted, running full tilt toward Janine and throwing her arms around her.

Janine took a quick step backward in an attempt to regain her balance so they wouldn't end up on the floor.

"You di'nt tell me yestiddy we was goin' to see Daddy today!"

"I know. I didn't know we were going to see your dad when you were at school. Even if I had known, we wouldn't have discussed it then."

"How come?"

This lovely heart-shaped box is richly detailed with cut-glass decorations, perfect for holding a precious memento or keepsake—and it's yours absolutely free when you accept our no-risk offer.

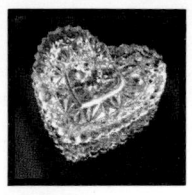

PLAY "LUCKY 7"

**Just scratch off the silver box with a coin.
Then check below to see which gifts you get.**

YES! I have scratched off the silver box. Please send me all the gifts for which I qualify. I understand I am under no obligation to purchase any books, as explained on the opposite page.

326 CIS AGM9
(C-SIL-D-10/92)

NAME

ADDRESS   APT

CITY   PROVINCE   POSTAL CODE

7	7	7	WORTH FOUR FREE BOOKS, FREE HEART-SHAPED CURIO BOX AND MYSTERY BONUS
🍒	🍒	🍒	WORTH FOUR FREE BOOKS AND MYSTERY BONUS
●	●	●	WORTH THREE FREE BOOKS
🔔	🔔	🍒	WORTH TWO FREE BOOKS

SILHOUETTE "NO RISK" GUARANTEE

- You're not required to buy a single book—ever!
- You must be completely satisfied or you may cancel at any time simply by sending us a note or a shipping statement marked "cancel" or returning any shipment to us at our cost. Either way, you will receive no more books; you'll have no obligation to buy.
- The free books and gifts you receive from this "Lucky 7" offer remain yours to keep no matter what you decide.

If offer card is missing, write to: Silhouette Reader Service, P.O. Box 609, Fort Erie, Ontario L2A 5X3

DETACH AND MAIL CARD TODAY

"Because when we're at school, I'm your teacher. Away from school I'm your friend."

"How come you can't be both all the time?"

"Well, I guess I can. I suppose the difference is what we talk about. At school we only talk about school things."

She could see Trisha mulling that one around in her head, which gave Janine a moment's breathing space. Five-year-olds were notorious for asking questions. Even though she was accustomed to the constant barrage for information, she wasn't always prepared to give comprehensive answers at a moment's notice.

"I take it you're ready to go?"

"Uh-huh. I been ready a lo-o-ong time!"

Janine laughed. "Then let's get on the road, young 'un."

The drive to the city was filled with happy chatter. Janine discovered that Trisha seldom visited her father there. He generally came to the ranch, so she was excited at the prospect of visiting his place again and seeing if he had changed anything since her last visit.

While Janine listened, she mentally prepared herself to stay in the background and not distract either of the Callaways from their visit. She rehearsed brief answers in her head as she followed the directions Cameron had given her to his place on the north side of the city.

As soon as she pulled to a stop in front of the building, all her rehearsed lines swept out of her head. Trisha was already excitedly recognizing various things from her last visit. By the time they were out of the car, the little girl was tugging Janine's hand to get her to hurry.

Cameron answered on the first ring, which was one of her worries answered; she had been afraid he might not be there and then she would have had to figure out what to do to entertain Trisha until he arrived to let them inside.

"Daddy!"

Cameron swooped his daughter into his arms. Trisha wrapped her arms around his neck and gave him quick kisses on his cheek, ear and jaw.

"It's good to see you, too, angel," he said in a gruff voice, hugging her to him. For a moment Janine forgot her self-consciousness and allowed herself to enjoy the scene before her—the tall lean man in jeans, checkered shirt and moccasins holding the little blond girl as though she were fragile glass, his face shining with love.

When he focused on Janine she felt as though a spotlight had been shone on her. She forced herself not to fidget.

"Thank you for bringing her," he said, holding out his hand. In a movement as natural as breathing, she placed her hand in his and allowed him to guide her into his home.

Once inside, she had to catch her breath. The place was nothing like she expected. Perhaps because he was alone, she had assumed that he would have a typical bachelor pad, messy and with minimal decorations. Instead, she could tell that he had put a great deal of thought into the decor to meet his own personal needs. The living area was open to the second story. A balcony hallway ran around three sides of it. The fourth wall was made entirely of glass. The view was of a secluded garden, enclosed for privacy by a stucco wall.

She could see a path wandering toward the back, disappearing behind the lush foliage. When he saw where she was looking, he said, "I have a pool out there. I try to spend at least an hour a day in the pool for exercise. I don't always manage it, though."

She turned away and noticed the cream colored walls, and the Southwestern motif, with its touches of peach, turquoise and copper. "I made reservations for dinner." He looked at his daughter, still in his arms. "Are you hungry?" She nodded vigorously and he laughed. "Me, too." Once again his intent gaze focused on Janine. "You're looking very springlike tonight. I like that color on you."

She couldn't stop the silly grin she knew she was wearing. She couldn't believe how wonderful it was to see him again, to have him notice what she wore and comment on it, to be there in his home.

"Thank you."

"I need to run upstairs and change. I dress very casually for work on Saturdays, but if I'm going to be taking my two favorite ladies out to dinner, then I want to look my best." He set the giggling Trisha on her feet, then went up the wrought-iron staircase to the second floor. He glanced down at Janine. "Go ahead and look around if you like."

She peeked through one of the open doors off the living room and found a very comfortable-looking study with a large desk and chair, a computer, fax machine, copier and a wall of bookcases filled to overflowing.

Next she saw a small dining room that connected to a kitchen filled with the latest cooking devices. The counter extended into a bar where he had obviously left some of the work he'd had with him earlier.

"Ya wanna see upstairs?"

Trisha had been following her from room to room. "Would you like to show me?"

"Uh-huh." She took Janine's hand and led her up the stairs, then turned right where Cameron had turned left. She took her all the way around the balcony to the last door, then opened it dramatically. "This—" she paused impressively "—is my room. Daddy let me help decorate it. I picked out the paper on the wall and the furniture and everything."

The French Provincial furniture made the room look as if it belonged to royalty. The canopy and its ruffled edge was in the same pattern as the border print that encircled the room.

"This is beautiful," Janine said slowly, taking it all in.

Trisha walked to a door and flung it open. "I have my own bathroom and everything." She walked through the bathroom and paused in front of another door. "'Course this door goes into the other room for the person who stays here, see?" She held open the door. "For guests and things."

Janine peered in and saw a room done in quiet good taste. When they were back on the balcony, Trisha pointed and said, "All of that over there is my daddy's room. It's bigger 'n big, my uncle Cody says. Do you wanna see?"

"Uh, no, Trisha, I don't think that would be a good idea. Your dad's getting dressed in there, and I don't think he would appreciate it if he had visitors."

Trisha covered her mouth with both hands, but couldn't disguise her giggles. Finally she burst out with, "Wouldn't it be funny if we walked in and he was nekkid?"

Janine could feel her cheeks heating up and fought to control her voice. "I doubt if he would find it funny at all."

At that moment Cameron came out of his room, buckling his belt. "What wouldn't I find funny?" he asked, meeting them in front of the stairs.

"Nothing, really," Janine hastened to say.

"I said if we was to walk in your room while you was puttin' on your clothes, we'd find you nekkid." Trisha giggled. "Wouldn't that be funny?"

"'Funny' isn't the word that immediately pops into my head," he said, obviously noting Janine's reddened cheeks. How she hated that betraying trait. She felt even more embarrassed when he winked at her.

Cameron picked up Trisha in one arm and held out his hand to Janine. They walked down the stairs and out through the kitchen to the garage, where his car was parked.

She was able to regain her composure on the way to the restaurant because Trisha kept Cameron occupied answering her numerous questions. It was nice to see someone else dealing with a constant barrage of questions. She smiled to herself, but Cameron caught it.

"Are you going to share what you find so amusing, or just sit over there, keeping your secrets?"

"No secrets, really. I can tell that you're used to answering her questions. You never have to search for an answer as I do. Sometimes she stumps me, I must admit."

He grinned. "Ah, but you see, I'm a trained trial lawyer. Cross-examination is a technique I learned years ago. Being the one cross-examined can get a little uncomfortable, of course, but it all goes with the territory."

"Well, I must commend you on how well you deal with her."

"Thank you, kindly, dear lady. I would have thought with your training that you would be used to it, too."

"Oh, I am. But the questions I get at school are considerably different than some she was throwing my way earlier today."

"Such as?"

"Well . . ."

Before she had to think of one, Trisha obligingly asked a new one. "Daddy, how come Missy Talbot's your dear lady?"

"That's just a figure of speech."

"What's a figure of speech?"

"Well, it's not to be taken literally."

"What's lit—"

"Okay, okay. You win. Let me try to explain a little differently. I was teasing Ms. Talbot. She is a lady and she is dear to me, so what I said was the truth, but put in a joking way."

"Oh."

Janine looked out the side window, afraid to face Cameron at the moment. Her heart had suddenly gone into double time when he said that she was dear to him. Dear God, what was happening here? She was already drawn to these people more than she cared to be. Somehow all her careful plans and ideas seemed to leave her whenever she was in close proximity to Cameron Callaway.

"Is something wrong?" he asked, and she quickly looked at him and forced herself to smile as casually as possible.

"Not a thing. Just looking forward to dinner."

"Good. I think Trisha might enjoy eating downtown along the river. There's some beautifully decorated outdoor places. We might go for a boat ride later, if you'd like." He glanced at Trisha.

"Oh, yes."

The evening went by in a blur of color, spicy, delicious food and lots of laughter. By the time they arrived home, Trisha was sound asleep.

"I have a suggestion to make," he said when they drove into his garage.

"Yes?"

"Why don't the two of you stay overnight and go back in the morning? There's no reason to rush back tonight, is there?"

"Other than we didn't bring any clothes for an overnight stay."

"Oh, Trisha has plenty of things here for her. I might be able to find you something to sleep in, though I'm afraid nothing of mine would fit you for day wear." His grin was filled with mischief when he added, "Unfortunately I don't know any women who might have left their clothes here."

Their eyes caught and held. Janine read the message in his. His eyes had haunted her every night this week and now here she was looking into them, being captivated by them once again.

"I suppose we could. I know you have a great deal to do tomorrow."

"Yes," he agreed. "But I decided to bring it home so that I can work here. I'll feed you breakfast and send you on your way."

"Won't your aunt be expecting Trisha and me tonight?"

"I'll give her a call once we get inside."

She shrugged. "Then we'll stay. Thank you."

He got out of the car and walked around to her side. Once he had the door open he leaned in to take Trisha from her arms. His fingers brushed against her breast, and both he and Janine froze for an instant before he picked up his daughter and carried her into the house. Janine slowly followed him, still tingling from his touch.

While he was upstairs, she found the coffee and made a pot. She didn't know about him, but she could definitely use a soothing beverage.

By the time he came downstairs she had poured them coffee and had carried it into the living room.

"A woman after my own heart," he said by way of greeting. "Thank you. I had intended to offer you something as soon as I got Miss Trisha down for the night."

"Did she ever wake up?"

"Not even by a flutter of an eyelash. That gal is out for the count."

She smiled, remembering the evening. "She had such a good time. I've never seen her eyes so big."

"I know. I hadn't realized how much she misses when I leave her at the ranch. She thoroughly enjoyed the mariachi band."

"Not to mention the Dixieland jazz."

"She must have walked for miles with us."

"I know. My legs were giving out before she began to wilt."

"But when she crashed, she crashed. One moment she was chattering like a magpie, the next minute she was asleep."

"I know. She has two speeds—flat-out and sound asleep."

They laughed softly and sipped their coffee. When they finished, Cameron took her cup and placed it on the coffee table next to his, then he applied a steady pressure on her hands to coax her to move closer to him. By the time he released her hands, they were side by side. That was when she realized that he had only released her so that he could place his arms around her.

"Thank you," he whispered, kissing her lightly on the mouth.

When she could think again, she said, "For what?"

"For bringing her to me. I would never have thought of it. I suppose I have a single-track mind. I knew I needed to work this weekend. It didn't occur to me that I could take a few hours and enjoy myself, as well."

"I'm glad you did. Enjoy yourself, I mean. It was good to see you laughing and relaxed."

"I'm only happy and relaxed around you, it seems."

She shook her head. "Not me. It's having Trisha here."

He took a lock of her hair and curled it around his finger. "It's true that I'm enjoying Trisha, but that's also because of you. As much as I love her, I have felt the obligation and responsibility of being her only parent more than I've been able to just relax and enjoy her as a child with her own personality and preferences. You've helped me get to know her better, and hopefully she's getting to know me better, as well."

"I'm glad. I think you'll both benefit from this."

He brushed her cheek with his forefinger. "Were you and your father close?"

Janine forced herself not to stiffen at his unwelcome question. After all, his curiosity was understandable. She just wished that she could give him a more positive answer.

"I never knew my father," she said in a low voice.

"Oh, I'm sorry. Was he killed in the service?"

She shook her head. "According to my mother, he was very upset when I was born and turned out to be a girl. There were some complications at the time of my birth. Both Mother and I almost died. When she finally recovered, the doctors told them she wouldn't be able to have any more children. So my dad left."

"Left? You mean he walked out?"

"According to my mother, he said he didn't want half a woman. He wanted a family. He had counted on having several boys. I don't know if he ever got them. Neither one of us ever heard from him again."

"Why that bast—"

She placed her fingers over his mouth. "No. There are many people out there who feel a family is extremely important."

"Well, of course family is important. But he had a family. How could he just walk away like that? I don't understand."

"Mother never fully recovered. As far back as I can remember she was always fragile. Perhaps it was just as well that he left. He didn't sound like the kind of person who had patience with anyone who did not have perfect health."

He hugged her. "That wasn't much of a life for you, if you had to look after your mother."

"I didn't know any other way to live so it seemed normal to me."

"Weren't you lonely?"

"Of course. But I learned to entertain myself."

"At least I had my parents until I was fifteen. They were there for me. And I had Cole and Cody. I can't imagine being on my own the way you were."

She touched his jaw, tracing a line from his ear to the corner of his mouth. "Thank you for caring. I really don't like to talk about my childhood."

"No, I can certainly see why. No wonder you teach kids. You're getting to enjoy what you never had growing up."

She shifted, always uncomfortable whenever her early life was the topic of discussion. "It's late. We both need our rest."

"I know, but I hate to let you go. Janine, you're becoming very important in my life, as well as Trisha's life."

She froze, hearing the husky intimacy of his voice. "Don't, Cam. Don't try to make something out of this. We're friends. Let's leave it like that."

"Friends, huh?" He nuzzled her ear, then bit the lobe. When she flinched he kissed it to make it better.

"Do you have any idea how much I want you in my bed?"

"Cam . . ." she began in a shaky voice.

"I know, I know. I'm still your host and you're still my guest and I'm not going to take advantage of you. But if my mama hadn't raised me to be such a gentleman, I'd sure as hell give it a try!"

She began to laugh, then hastily covered her mouth. "Well, in the interests of keeping your mama proud of her little boy, I'm going to bed and relieve you of some of your temptations."

"Thanks a lot."

"Don't mention it."

"So when will I see you again?" Cameron asked.

"When do you want to see me again?"

"As soon as possible," he admitted.

"I don't have much free time during the week."

"Neither do I." He was quiet for several minutes. "Maybe next weekend we could fly up to Arlington and spend the day at Six Flags."

"Fly?"

"Sure. Pete will fly us up. We'll get a car at the airport, spend the day, then fly home."

"Who's Pete?"

"Our pilot. He gets Cole and I around—to wherever we need to be in this state. It's too damned big to drive everywhere."

"You have your own private plane?"

"The company does. Actually I think there's two, plus a helicopter."

"When I'm with you and Trisha, I forget that you're part of the Callaways, and then when you say something like, 'Let's fly to Six Flags,' I'm jerked back into reality."

"Why? Is there something wrong with flying to Six Flags?"

"Not to you. You've always lived like that. I guess I find it difficult to understand why you work so hard when you obviously don't need the money."

"I work because it's my responsibility to help Cole keep everything going."

"But Cody doesn't feel the same obligation?"

"No. He's never been interested in any of it. Oh, he loves the ranch as we all do. But he goes his own way."

"Does he work at all?"

"Yeah, he does, but don't ask me what he does, because I don't know exactly. I know he's got contacts in high places. He's been helping me try to get to the bottom of some of the incidents in a few of our companies."

"But being a Callaway doesn't particularly impress you, does it?"

"Not particularly. Is it supposed to?"

She just shook her head, feeling helpless to explain.

"Does it bother *you?*" he finally asked.

"I'm not certain," she said, trying to be honest. "Your life-style is nothing like I'm used to."

"Do you think you could get used to it?"

She didn't like the seriousness in his voice. "I suppose I can be a friend to a Callaway." She grinned. "See, I'm not prejudiced!"

He grabbed her, pulling her onto his lap. "You deserve this and you know it," he growled and covered her mouth with his.

Once again, she felt almost as if she were melting. How had she allowed this man past her defenses? She didn't know when it had happened, or how it had happened. She just knew that she found him impossible to resist.

Six

Janine let herself into the kitchen of the small house she lived in, finally admitting that the Texas heat in August was too much for her. She had been working out in the postage-stamp-size backyard, encouraging her annuals to continue blooming by carefully watering them and removing the weeds.

Now she felt as limp as an overcooked noodle. She pulled off her gardening gloves and her sun hat, reached into the refrigerator and grabbed a large pitcher of iced tea. That in itself was a sure sign she was becoming an honest-to-God Texan. No self-respecting Texan would be caught in the summertime without plenty of iced tea.

She walked through the cool house and wandered out onto her front porch, which was shaded from the direct sunlight by an overgrown lilac bush. Even with the heat, there was generally a breeze. Today was no exception.

She sat on the porch swing, looking down at her shorts and sleeveless shirt in disgust. She looked like Pigpen, in the Charlie Brown comic strip. She would go shower and change as soon as she finished her glass of iced tea. For now, however, she intended to sit and rock, to take pleasure in her gardening accomplishments and dream of Cameron Callaway.

She had spent most of her idle time this summer dreaming of that man. School had been out for almost two months now, so she had more free time. She wasn't certain how it had come about, but most of her time had been taken up with Cameron and Trisha.

After their highly successful trip to Six Flags, they had made many outings around the state. Sometimes they visited places nearby, such as Breckenridge Park in San Antonio, or the zoo where Trisha got to ride an elephant. One time they took her to see Fort Sam Houston, where the inner section of the restored quadrangle had been turned into a wildlife preserve, almost a petting zoo.

Sometimes they went farther afield. One weekend they visited the Schlitterbahn Waterpark in New Braunsfels. Another time they drove to San Marcus to enjoy the Aquarena Springs water show. Cameron had gotten tickets for the touring production of Cats in Dallas, and they had flown up to see it.

Trisha had loved it all, but she begged to return to see the dolphins at Sea World after a visit there.

The summer had been an obvious success in many ways. Trisha had discovered how much she enjoyed being with her father. As for Janine . . . she had fallen in love.

For more than three months the trio had spent almost every weekend together. When Cameron's schedule was unusually hectic, they would stay at his home in San Antonio or go to the ranch.

He had left Trisha at the ranch during the summer but he was making plans to move her permanently to San Antonio in September so that she could start kindergarten there. He had suggested that Janine might help him interview a combination housekeeper/companion for Trisha. Only the most qualified women were interviewed and she had found two with promise, but for one reason or another, Cameron decided against each one.

Janine sipped her tea and smiled. Wouldn't she enjoy being the one who was there for Trisha every day? Of course the idea was more impossible now than ever. How could she possibly see Cameron as her boss?

There had been a couple of times during their association when she had stopped fighting herself and enjoyed the moment, much like that first dinner they'd had together last April at the ranch. She would have needed very little, if any, encouragement to have made love with him now, but he had never taken advantage of her momentary weaknesses.

Quite honestly, she was frightened to allow their relationship to change. What they were sharing was very precious to her. Cameron had become the brother she had never had—teasing and tormenting her, hugging and nurturing her, always there when she needed him. Other times he was the father she had always wanted—

intelligent, filled with wisdom and sound advice, understanding, undemanding, fully accepting her.

He had coaxed her out of the shell she had lived in all her life, making her believe that she had something of value to offer another person. He appeared to be happier when he was around her, and more relaxed. He laughed more easily.

So did she.

Since their relationship could never culminate into more than friendship, Janine didn't want to risk what they had by allowing them to become lovers. At the moment she could handle not only loving him, but being in love with him. But if she allowed their relationship to become more intimate, she stood a good chance of losing everything.

She wasn't willing to take the risk.

Thus far, Cameron had seemed to accept the limits she had set. She couldn't ask for more from a friend. What had been haunting her in recent weeks was the fact that *she* wanted more. How could that be? She had been shy around men all her life. It was as though they were alien beings whose actions were incomprehensible to her. By the time she reached high school she had spent most of her spare time studying at the library and reading fiction.

Until she met Bobby. He had pursued her with a single-mindedness that the sixteen-year-old girl she had been could neither ignore nor resist.

She took another sip of her tea and sighed. How strange. Today was the first time she had been able to think of Bobby with a sense of detachment. What had happened had not been his fault. A driver who had lost control of his car had veered into their lane and hit them. Bobby had done everything he could to avoid the oncoming car. She later heard that the police had commended him on his quick reflexes, which had kept them from going off the road and down the steep gully nearby.

They had been such kids back then. It was time for her to let go of the emotions that surrounded her memories of Bobby. He had chosen to break up their relationship after the accident, based on who he was and what he wanted from life. She could understand much better now that his decision had been the best thing for both of them.

She smiled to herself. Cameron had brought real healing into her life. Someday maybe she could explain to him what had happened to her during that traumatic time in her life and how severely her life had been changed. Never before had she believed she could look back with such a sense of acceptance of her situation. Having Cameron in her life had made such a wonderful difference.

A car pulled up in front of her house, and she idly glanced toward the street. She rarely received company—not unless they called first—so she knew that whoever had stopped was either lost and looking for directions or was visiting one of her neighbors.

Her eyes widened and she groaned, remembering how she looked. It was Cameron! He was already on his way up the sidewalk. When he saw her looking his way he waved. Darn. She didn't have time to slip inside and get cleaned up. Slowly she came to her feet.

"Hello, pretty lady," he said with a grin. "How've ya been?"

She glanced down ruefully at her dirt-smudged shorts and top and her bare feet. "As you can see, I've been gardening. You'll be pleased to know that I left some of the dirt for the flowers." She looked out at the car and saw that it was empty. "What brings you this far south in the middle of the week?"

He sank down on the swing and tugged her to join him. "I realized at about eleven o'clock this morning that I've been working too hard."

She grinned. "And what bolt of lightning managed to get your attention?"

He leaned against the chain holding the swing, closed his eyes and sighed. "I dunno, exactly. I woke up this morning with a god-awful headache after another restless night. I had trouble concentrating on my work all morning. Finally I told my secretary I was going to take a few days off for a little R and R."

"So you're going to the ranch, I take it?"

He opened his eyes and looked at her, his gaze seeming to burn into her. "No. I came to see you."

His timing couldn't have been worse. She was already in a very vulnerable position because she had finally consciously admitted to herself that she loved him.

"So how's your headache now?"

He closed his eyes once more. "It feels like a dozen buzz saws working at high speed," he admitted wearily.

"Would you like some iced tea and aspirin?"

"Sounds good," he murmured. "It just feels good to sit here with you and rest for a few minutes."

She went into the house and found the necessary pain relievers, then poured him a glass of tea. She was more worried than she let on. In all the time she had known him, Cameron had never taken off in the middle of the day like this. Beneath his deep tan, he looked pale.

When she returned to the porch she discovered he hadn't moved. "Cameron?"

"Mmm?"

"Why don't you take these and lie down for a while, give them a chance to work."

He seemed to open his eyes with difficulty. "Sure," he mumbled. "Whatever you say." He got to his feet and swayed. She handed him the tablets and drink and watched as he swallowed them. He had obviously gone home and changed before heading south. He no longer wore what he laughingly called his lawyer uniform—a suit. Instead he was in faded jeans, a lightweight cotton shirt and moccasins.

Impulsively she took his hand. As soon as she touched him, she blurted out, "Cam, you're burning up!"

"No wonder," he muttered, following her into the house, "It's hot as hell out there." He paused in the front room of her small house. "Now this is more like it, darlin'. Much better."

She led him into her bedroom and hastily removed the bedspread. "There you go. See if you can relax and rest."

Like a child, Cameron docilely sat on the side of the bed and slipped off his shoes, then wearily lay back on the pillow. "Mmm. Your pillow smells like you—like flowers and fresh air and sunshine."

She turned away, too touched by his comment to respond. She closed the blinds on both the windows so that the room lay in shadow, then pulled the chain of the large paddle fan in the center of the ceiling.

When she looked at Cameron again, he already seemed to be asleep. She leaned over and touched his forehead. He felt very hot and dry. Something was wrong, but she didn't know what more she could do. Maybe he would feel better after a nap.

In the meantime she would take a shower and change, then make them something cool to eat for supper.

Two hours later Janine was in the kitchen when she heard the bathroom door close. She realized that Cameron was finally awake. She waited for several minutes, and when he didn't come out she became worried. Walking into the hall she said, "Cam? Are you all right?"

She heard a muffled sound.

"Cam?" When she heard him groan she opened the door. He was sitting on the side of the tub, his head in his hands. "Do you still have your headache?" she asked sympathetically.

He stared at her in surprise and confusion. "Janine? What are you doing here?"

She thought he was teasing her. "I didn't mean to barge in on you, but I heard you groan and thought you might need something."

He glanced around the small room in bewilderment. "Where am I?"

Janine became truly alarmed. "Why don't you lie down again, Cam? Will you do that for me?" She walked over and coaxed him to stand, then slid her arms around his waist.

He was so weak he could scarcely walk. By the time she got him back to the side of her bed, her muscles were trembling from the exertion.

"Damn, it's hot," he muttered, and before she could stop him he'd stripped off his pants and shirt. He stretched out on the bed with a sigh and closed his eyes.

Janine's eyes were drawn to the only part of his body that remained covered—by a pair of navy briefs that gave new meaning to the word "brief."

It wasn't as though she had never seen him un-clothed before. The three of them had spent a great deal of time this summer in his pool. But this was different somehow. More personal.

She turned away and went to her linen closet, found another sheet and draped it across his body. He didn't stir. Then she went to the phone and called the ranch. When Rosie answered, Janine asked to speak to Letty. After a few moments, Letty picked up the phone and asked, "Yes? Who is it?"

Janine smiled. Letty had always reminded her of the woman who lived next door to her when she was growing up. The woman had been a cantankerous old bat, yelling at all the neighborhood children if they encroached on her property even an inch. But when Janine's mother had gotten so much worse, it had been her neighbor who had come to care for her while Janine was in school each day.

"Letty, this is Janine. I need your advice."

"What about?"

"Do you have a family doctor?"

"What's the matter? You sick?"

"No, I'm not. But Cameron stopped by earlier today on his way to the ranch. He wasn't feeling well, so I gave him some aspirin and suggested he rest. When he woke up a few minutes ago, he couldn't seem to remember coming here at all. He's very hot to the touch. I think we need to get a doctor to him."

"Humph. You won't find any of those new doctors botherin' with house calls, I'll tell you that. Fred Whitney's been retired for more than five years, but he's still as sharp as they come. I'll get hold of him and tell him to go check on Cameron. Give me your address."

Janine felt relief shoot through her. Letty was going to help. She quickly gave her the address and hung up, then returned to check on Cameron. He hadn't moved.

She went to the kitchen and dished up some of the chicken salad she had made for their supper, knowing she had to eat something. Then she paced between the kitchen and the living room, ending each loop at the front door, staring out at the street. When a well-kept older sedan slid to a stop in front of the house, she gave a sigh of relief and opened the door.

The man getting out of the car must have been a commanding figure at one time. He was tall, but spare, with a shock of white hair and the keenest blue eyes she had ever seen.

"You must be Janine Talbot," he said when he stepped up onto her porch carrying a bag.

"Yes, sir, I am. And you're Dr. Whitney."

"Well, yes, that's what my diploma says, but folks around here have been callin' me Dr. Fred for more years than I care to remember."

She smiled. "Dr. Fred it is, then."

"So where is that young 'un, anyway? I haven't seen Cam in a coon's age. I was always having to patch him up for one thing or another when he was growing up. Did he ever tell you 'bout the time he fell out of the hayloft in the barn and broke his arm?"

She was ahead of him in the hallway. She stopped when she came to the bedroom door and nodded toward the bed. "No, I'm afraid he's never mentioned it."

"Not surprising. Got his backside tanned good for that one, broken arm or no. That loft was off-limits to those kids." He walked over to a straight-back chair and pulled it toward the bed. He sat down and took Cam's wrist between his fingers. Then he removed his stethoscope from his bag, slipped the ear plugs into his ears with the ease of long practice and held the other end to Cameron's chest.

Janine stood at the end of the bed and watched helplessly. The doctor continued to move the shiny disk around on Cameron's chest and listen...move and listen...until she thought she would scream with impatience.

Finally he removed the stethoscope. "Cameron? Wake up, son, and talk to me."

She watched with fascination as Cameron first frowned, then slowly opened his eyes. He stared at the doctor in confusion. "Dr. Fred?" he whispered through dry lips. "What are you doin' here?"

The doctor smiled. "Checkin' up on you, son. This young lady thought you might need some help."

Cameron's eyes wandered from the doctor to Janine. He gave her a lazy smile but didn't say anything.

"Cameron, how long have you been feeling poorly?"

"A long time," he said, closing his eyes.

The doctor grinned at Janine before turning back to Cameron. "Does that mean years, days or hours? I need you to be more specific if you can."

"I don't know, doc. A couple of days, maybe. Haven't had much energy. My throat's been bothering me."

"Let me see," he said, pulling out a small instrument with a light.

Cameron obligingly opened his mouth.

"Uh-huh."

Cameron shut his mouth and his eyes. Janine couldn't be quite so relaxed about the procedure.

"Do you know what's wrong?" she finally asked.

"Well, I suppose I could order up a bunch of tests, get some cultures, take blood samples, or I could tell you what I suspect based on years of experience."

"What do you think?"

"First of all, this boy's been pushing himself too hard for too long. Now you can't expect a body to receive that kinda treatment without it decidin' sooner or later to rebel. I suspect that Cam's body just decided to present him with its bill. Because he's rundown, it's my guess that he picked up the current virus that's all the rage in the medical journals and running around in all the doctors' offices. He's got all the symptoms."

"What can we do?"

He smiled at her use of the plural pronoun, making her aware of how possessive she sounded toward Cameron.

"Well, I could give him some antibiotics to take, and something for the pain and fever. But the absolute, most important thing he needs is rest, and I doubt he's going to want to do that much, knowing Cam the way I do. The minute he starts feeling a mite stronger, he's goin' to be pushing to get back to work."

"And if he does?"

Fred shrugged. "No predictin', of course. But this is a hardy li'l old virus. People who get up too soon are relapsing, usually much sicker than the first go round. Those are the ones they're puttin' in the hospitals."

"How long would you recommend he stay in bed?"

"Absolute minimum . . . a week. Ten days would be even better."

"How contagious is this virus?"

"No more than most. Why? You afraid to catch it?"

She smiled. "Not me. But I thought about having his daughter, Trisha, visit a little later when he's feeling better."

He shook his head. "Not until his fever's down. Little ones are cute and all that, but they drain a person right fast. Give him a chance to get his strength back first."

She nodded. "All right."

The doctor stood and stared down at Cameron. "The man's exhausted. Just look at him. I know the fever and infection didn't help, but part of this is just plain neglect." He shook his head. "People nowadays trash their bodies, then wonder why they quit working on 'em. Darndest thing I've ever seen. Then they want a bunch of pills to swallow and expect that to fix 'em up all right and tight, ready to keep running. It just don't work that way.''

"I know." She started for the door. "Would you like something to drink before you leave?"

"Don't mind if I do, thank you. Oh, and if you'll show me where you keep your phone, I'll call in some prescriptions and have Oliver down at the drugstore deliver them.''

Her eyes widened. "They'll do that?"

The old man grinned. "For certain people they will.''

By the time he hung up the phone, Janine had poured his tea. "I made chicken salad to feed Cam before I realized how sick he was. Could I tempt you into eating some?"

Fred glanced at her in surprise, then smiled. "Now, how did you know I do most of my own cookin' these days?"

"I didn't.''

"Well, then you made a darned brilliant guess. I never bother with stuff I have to chop and slice, not if I can help it. Your salad looks mighty appetizing.''

"Then have a seat and I'll fix us each a plate.''

She also brought out the fresh vegetable salad she had placed in the refrigerator earlier. They sat down and began to get better acquainted.

Fred Whitney had known the Callaways for years and had delivered the youngest two boys. He was filled with tales about the family, the land and some of the history of the area. Janine found him fascinating.

More than two hours passed before he reluctantly took his leave. He gave her instructions about what to feed Cameron, what not to feed him and how to deal with a grouchy patient. She felt warmed and accepted by the kindly old man. He started down the steps. "Oh, I almost forgot. Letty told me to be sure to let her know what was wrong with Cameron. I'd just as soon not have to talk to the old bat myself if you'd like to call." Since he'd already told her of several battles the two extremely opinionated and self-willed people had had, she wasn't surprised at his comment.

"I'd be glad to, Dr. Fred."

"I'll be around sometime tomorrow to check on our fella in there. If you need me before then, just give me a call at that number I gave you."

Because the doctor had been there when the medicine arrived, he had showed her how to give Cameron the necessary dosage. Speaking clearly and firmly, he had had Cameron sit up and take the tablets, then swallow them with water. She hoped she could be as firm.

She went back in and called Letty. As soon as the woman recognized her voice, she said, "What in tarnation is goin' on? Did you have to hospitalize him? It's been hours since you called."

"Uh, no. Dr. Fred said he was all right here, so long as I make sure he takes his medication on time. He thinks he's contracted a flu virus."

"I'm not surprised. Everybody I know seems to be coming down with something these days."

"Yes. The doctor thinks that Cameron's is a little more severe because he's run-down."

"Of course he's run-down. He skips meals, smokes too much, seldom sleeps more than four hours a night. What does he expect?"

"Well, he seems to be resting okay for the moment."

"If you want, I could send some of the hands into town and bring him out here. It won't be the first time he's had to convalesce at the ranch."

"I don't think moving him would be a good idea. Besides, I'm home all day now. I don't mind looking after him."

"You sure?"

"Positive."

"Well, okay, then. But if it gets to be too much for you, you just hollar, you hear?"

Janine smiled at Letty's tone and choice of words. "I hear."

"I'll let Cole know what's going on. He and Cam work closely together."

"Oh! I'd forgotten all about his work. Yes, thank you. I'm sure Cameron will be relieved to know his brother knows where he is."

"Tell him I'll be in one of these days to check on him. That'll get him out of bed in a hurry," Letty said.

"I'll do that. Thanks for everything, Letty. You've been a big help."

"That's what family's for, young lady."

Janine hung up the phone and went in to check on Cameron. Since she had never had a family other than her mother, she didn't know what a family was for. She had never missed what she had never had. However, it felt good to know that there was someone to call when she needed help.

She didn't feel alone anymore.

Seven

There were flames shooting up all around him. He fought his way through the smoke and haze, trying to get away from the searing blast of heat that engulfed him. He had to find relief. He had to escape before—

There. There was the voice, calling to him. He recognized the sound of that voice—it offered coolness and a refreshing balm. If only he could find it. He continued to struggle on, a sense of desperation forcing him to fight until the smoke and the haze lightened and he saw her standing beside the gurgling stream, beckoning to him. He broke into a lumbering uneven gait, exhausted from his struggles. He stumbled toward her, knowing that if he could just reach her he would be all right.

"Raise your head, Cam, and drink this."

He felt a glass at his lips, then felt the cool water trickle over their parched surface.

"Here. Swallow these. They'll help."

His throat ached from smoke inhalation, but he forced himself to swallow. He was rewarded with more water. The flames began to die down, their heat lessening.

Then she placed him in the cooling stream and bathed him with the comforting water. Her hands soothed his body, stroking the heat away, leaving him relaxed and at ease. He drifted off, sinking deeper and deeper into the healing water.

Cam jerked awake, his eyes flying open. He was in a bedroom, but an unfamiliar one. It seemed small, from the little he could see in the dim light from a lamp beside the bed.

Blinds covered the two windows.

Where the hell was he?

He couldn't remember a damned thing. He raised himself on his elbow and a pain shot through his head. He groaned, certain his head was going to topple off his shoulders.

"Cam? Are you all right?"

He moved his head carefully toward the door where the familiar voice came from and squinted. "Janine?"

She floated toward him, wearing something long and flowing. "Is your head still hurting?"

An understatement. "Yeah."

She poured more water from a pitcher on the bedside table into a glass. She opened a vial and took out a tablet. "Here. Maybe this will help." She handed him the medicine. As soon as he placed it on his tongue she handed him the glass, then wrapped her fingers around his to guide it to his mouth.

The water was cool and refreshing. He drained the glass, then allowed himself to sink back into the bed again. "What am I doing here?" he mumbled, surprised at how disagreeable he sounded.

She smiled at him. "At the moment, you're fighting a virus."

"How long have I been here?"

She glanced at her wristwatch. "About twelve hours."

Why couldn't he remember? He last recalled being at the office. The whole thing was too complicated to work out. He closed his eyes, then suddenly realized that he hadn't thanked her for taking care of him. "Thank you," he said gruffly.

He could hear amusement in her voice when she replied, "You're welcome."

Cameron was sweltering. He pushed off the covers but someone kept replacing them. "It's too damned hot. Get those blasted things off me!"

"You'll become chilled without them. Lie still, please. I'll get you something to drink."

"I don't want anything to drink. I want to get rid of the covers!"

The hands moved away. "Go ahead, then. Have it your way."

He felt exceedingly proud of himself. He had won the battle with the sweet-voiced witch. He shoved them away, feeling the cool breeze touch his body, moving across him . . . touching, tingling, chilling him until he began to shake.

The covers suddenly appeared from somewhere, falling softly around him, protecting him, nurturing him, caring for him. He smiled to himself in pleased satisfaction and allowed himself to drift off again.

The next time he opened his eyes, the room was still coolly shaded from the bright light on the other side of the window blinds. The lamp beside the bed was off. He tossed the covers aside and lowered his legs to the floor. They were made of lead. He could scarcely move.

New determination caused him to reach for the bedpost at the end of the bed and haul himself upright. Only by hanging on to furniture and bracing himself against walls did he make it to the bathroom door. After relieving himself, he stared into the mirror over the sink in dismay. What the hell? He looked as though he'd been on a five-day drunk. He needed a shave, his hair stood on end and his eyes were bloodshot. There was a steady pounding in his head.

He grasped the doorknob and jerked it open, only to find his way barred.

"What are you doing out of bed?"

He stared at Janine in bewilderment. He hadn't seen her this angry since the first day he had met her. Her eyes were shooting sparks.

"Hi." He gave her his most endearing smile. It had no effect on her whatsoever.

"Dr. Fred said that you were not to get up for any reason. So get back in bed. Now."

"I had to go to the bathroom."

"Oh."

Ha! That shut her up. Her cheeks pinkened, which made her eyes look greener. He could feel his knees slowly buckling. Unless he wanted to collapse at her feet, he knew he was going to have to follow her orders.

Only then did he become aware that he was nude.

"What the hell! Where are my clothes?" He lurched toward the bedroom and made his way to the bed.

"You took off most of them when you went to bed," she said, following him into the room. She leaned against the doorway and crossed her arms. "I took off your briefs last night when I was sponging you off, trying to bring your fever down. Letty is supposed to have someone drop off some more clothes for you in a day or so."

He had climbed under the sheet and had it bunched in his lap during her casual explanation. "A day or so! I need my clothes now!"

Her smile was consoling but firm. "No. You're far from over this. You have four more days of heavy-duty antibiotics."

"I don't have to stay in bed to take them, for God's sake."

"Oh, yes. These particular kind plainly state that you must stay in bed or they won't work."

He studied her suspiciously, but she didn't crack a smile. "I never heard of such a thing."

She shrugged. "It's a new kind of medication. However, you can eat something if you like. Are you hungry?"

He thought about that for a few moments, allowing himself to slowly sink back onto the bed. "Not really," he said.

"I've made some chicken broth for you. Why don't you try a cup?"

He nodded, then watched her disappear from the doorway. Damn, he couldn't remember a time when he had felt at such a disadvantage. He felt like something that had been dragged behind a horse for a few days, then left out in the sun. Meanwhile, she looked as cool as an ice queen, standing there in her shorts and matching blouse, her hair high on her head in some sort of topknot.

She returned with a tray holding a cup and a glass of iced tea. She placed the cup beside the bed, took the tea and sat down in a rocker he hadn't noticed before.

"I feel like a fool," he muttered, reaching for the cup of broth.

"Why?"

"I shouldn't be here, making you wait on me like this. I can't imagine why I came here if I was feeling so rotten."

"You don't remember." She made the comment as a statement, not a question.

He shook his head, carefully sipping on the broth.

"You said you were having trouble concentrating because of a bad headache, so decided to leave work. You stopped by here on the way to the ranch."

"Why didn't you send me on?"

"It never occurred to me. I'm sorry if you're uncomfortable being here. Letty offered to send someone to pick you up, but I talked her out of it."

He eyed her across the top of his cup. "You mean you *wanted* to look after me?"

Her grin caught him off guard. "Amazing, isn't it? I must enjoy being called a series of unprintable names."

"I did that?"

She nodded.

"I'm sorry."

"Don't worry. I don't intend to hold it against you. You've been pretty sick, Cam. And you're not out of the woods yet."

"Nonsense. I'm feeling much better. Just a little weak, maybe. As soon as I have some clothes I'll—"

"You'll stay in bed and rest."

"But—"

"No arguments. Why don't you take some more of your medication so I don't have to disturb you with it in another half hour or so?"

Where had she gotten such an air of command? He'd almost found himself saluting her. When she handed him the tablets, he immediately swallowed them.

"Well, maybe I'll rest for a few minutes. Then I'll call Letty and . . ." He closed his eyes and was hardly aware of the empty cup slipping out of his hand. She took it from him, and he smiled as he sank deeper into the pillow. Just a few minutes' more rest. That was all he needed.

When Dr. Fred arrived, Janine met him at the front door before he had a chance to knock. "How's our patient today?" he asked with a smile.

"Anything *but* patient, I'm afraid. He's already demanding his clothes."

Fred guffawed. "Then he really must be sick, if all he can think about around a beautiful gal like you is getting his clothes *on!*"

"He got out of bed this morning while I was in the kitchen. When I found him he was so weak he could barely stand but that didn't stop him from giving me a hard time.''

"What was he doing out of bed?"

"Answering nature's call."

"Ah. Well, it's too much to hope for that he'd allow you to attend to everything. So I suppose I'll relent and allow him bathroom privileges. But that's all. Is he awake now?"

"You can check, but I don't think so. He fell asleep in the middle of a sentence."

Fred chuckled. "Good, good. Just what he needs. I'll admit the pain reliever I prescribed is strong enough to knock him out." He patted her on the shoulder. "I'll just take a peek, anyway."

She watched from the doorway as Dr. Fred found his chair, sat down and took Cameron's wrist. Cameron didn't flinch. Then the doctor listened to his chest, checked his eyes and throat without awakening him. When he was finished, he patted Cameron's head gently.

Dr. Fred's eyes were twinkling when he came out of the bedroom. "He's already improved tremendously, thanks to you. His color is much better. He's still running a fever, but it's down considerably from yesterday. All and all, I'd say he's mending nicely."

"I gave him some homemade chicken broth. He didn't seem very hungry."

"That's all right. Just continue to keep the food light. His body will know when it's ready to take on more nourishment. If we listened to our bodies more, we'd stay a lot healthier. You're doing a fine job looking after him, by the way."

"Thank you."

"He's a very fortunate young man, you know. Not too many of us get lucky twice in this life."

Janine didn't understand what he was talking about and her confusion must have shown on her face. "My wife, Trudy, died almost fifteen years ago. I never found anyone that came close to taking her place. I'm glad that young Cameron found you. He's too young to spend the rest of his life alone."

"Oh, but, Dr. Fred, we're just friends."

He smiled and let himself out the front door. "Of course you are. That's the very best kind." She watched him walk out to his car and get in, then carefully drive away.

The bright lights suddenly flashed in front of him. He swerved, trying to miss them, fighting not to lose control. He heard a scream as the lights filled the windshield, and then he began to spin and spin, the lights flashing, the scream going on and on and on . . .

"Cam! Cam, honey. Wake up. You're dreaming, Cam. It's all right. It's just a dream."

He fought his way out of the noise and confusion, forcing his way up out of the nightmare. He could feel cool hands soothing his face and shoulders. He clutched at them, feeling their solidness, relief rushing over him when he discovered she was real. She was there beside him, holding him, loving him.

"Janine?" When he opened his eyes he realized that she hadn't turned on a light.

"Yes, Cam, it's me. I'm sorry to awaken you. I heard you groaning and muttering and knew you must have been dreaming."

She was on the side of the bed. He had his arms around her. He gave a tug so that she toppled against him. He shifted, pulling her down beside him. "What are you doing?" she said with a muffled laugh.

"I knew it was you," he said slowly, still coming to grips with the knowledge.

"Well, yes. There's no one else here."

"No. I mean, even in the midst of the nightmare I recognized your voice immediately and knew that if I fought to get to you, I'd be all right." He held her to him, smoothing his hand over the back of her head. When she didn't say anything, he asked, "Where are you sleeping?"

"On the couch." Her voice was very quiet.

"Then I'm in your bed, aren't I?"

"I don't mind."

"Aren't there two bedrooms?"

"I use the other bedroom for storage and hobbies and things. I never bothered to furnish it with a bed. I didn't need one."

"I'm sorry you had to give yours up."

"I'm not." He could hear the sound of her smile in her voice. "Are you hungry?" she asked after a moment.

"A little."

"Let me get you something. You'll probably sleep better." She waited, but he didn't let go of her. She felt too good to him, held close in his arms like that. Then she pressed her palm against his chest in an effort to pull away, and he reluctantly let go of her.

She left the room without turning on the light. He was content, lying in the dark, waiting for her. When she returned she flicked on the small light beside the bed and handed him a cup of something steaming and fragrant.

"I didn't wake you to take your next dose of medicine. You were sleeping so peacefully I didn't have the heart. But you can take it now." She gave him the tablets, then slipped out of the room.

When he finished the broth he decided that she might not intend to come back into the room. He started to get up, then remembered his lack of clothes. Frustrated, he draped the sheet around himself and stood.

Irritated by his lack of strength, he made his way into the bathroom. He knew a shower would help him, so he threw off the sheet and climbed into the tub. Standing beneath the soothing spray helped to ease the aches that invaded his body. By the time he finished, he felt better, but knew that he wouldn't be able to run any races any time soon. He was already yearning for bed again.

When he walked back into the bedroom, this time with a large bath towel around his waist, he discovered that Janine had returned. Not only had she retrieved his dishes, she had also changed the sheets and made the bed. However, she was nowhere in sight.

Already feeling the trembling setting into his muscles, he turned off the light, tossed the towel aside and crawled thankfully into bed. Within moments he was asleep.

Janine lay awake on the couch for a long time, thinking. Perhaps she had been foolish to insist he stay there with her. Given the attraction they had for each other, wasn't she asking for trouble? At first he had been too ill for it to matter, but she could see that he was rapidly improving. Perhaps tomorrow she would suggest that he get a ride out to the ranch. Or, she could take him there if he wished.

Yes. That would be the best thing—for both of them—regardless of what her heart was telling her.

She was still awake when she heard him moan, and she guessed that his nightmare was back. Without hesitation she ran into the other room to bring him out of the mind-numbing terror that seemed to lurk in his dreams.

"Cam? It's okay, Cam. It's just a dream." She leaned over him, touching his brow.

With no warning, his hands grabbed her wrists and he jerked her forward, pulling her off balance. With a squeak of dismay, she tried to fall away from him, not wanting to startle him awake with her sudden weight on top of him. She twisted and rolled so that she landed on the bed beside him. Only then did she become aware that he had kicked off his sheet and was lying there nude beside her.

Before she could pull away he placed one of his muscular thighs across her hips, pinning her to the bed.

"Cam? It's me, Janine. Wake up, Cam, please." She spoke the words in a low voice, still hoping not to jar him awake.

"Janine," he mumbled.

"Yes, wake up now."

He released her wrists, but she still couldn't move. She placed her palm on his chest. He was too warm, obviously still running a fever. He stroked his hand across her body, then paused, fingering the cotton nightgown she wore.

"Wha' are you doin' in this?" he muttered, slurring his words. He reached down and grabbed the hem, then lifted the gown up over her head. It was still caught on the shoulder closest to him. "Hmm, that's better," he murmured. Once again he ran his hand over her body, from the top of her thighs to her throat, then back again. The second time he circled her breast, teased the crest with his fingers, then leaned over and placed his mouth over the aroused tip.

She stiffened at the unfamiliar sensation, then shuddered as a multitude of new feelings ran through her, turning her body to molten metal.

He shifted, nudged her legs apart with his thigh, and with a sigh she relaxed into the pleasure of feeling him pressed so intimately against her. His thigh was rhythmically moving against her. When he shifted his attention to her other breast she moaned and squirmed slightly, feeling an ache she had never known before.

He seemed to understand her bewilderment, because he finally touched her where the ache was centered, softly rubbing the tips of his fingers across the exact spot.

She arched with his hand, relishing in the delightful sensation. When he raised his head and kissed her, she thought there must be steam coming from both of them. She held him tightly, afraid to let go. Her hands slowly moved up and down his back, down to his muscled buttocks, then returned to the slight indentation of his spine. Then Cameron tugged her gown from her arm and shoulder and tossed it out of the way.

She reveled in each new explosion of feeling he provoked. His restless hands moved over her body, tantalizing her until she thought she would explode. By the time he hovered over her, she wanted to leap on him and hold him fast against her heat.

There was no embarrassment, no fear. This was Cameron, the man she loved, the man who could drive her to distraction with just one look... Cameron... Cam...

Yes, just there. That was where the ache had first appeared and grown more intense. She caught herself holding her breath, wanting him so desperately, as he slowly pushed against her, creating more and more pressure until she was filled with the need, with him, with—

A sharp pain brought her partway out of the sensory place of wonder. She stiffened, but before she could protest, his mouth found hers once more and she realized that he was pressed firmly against her and fully inside. He leaned on his forearms on each side of her head and bathed her face in soft kisses, soothing her, calming her. In the deep shadows of the room, she couldn't see his face. But she could feel him as he lay against her so intimately.

He nibbled on her bottom lip, sucked on it slightly, then stroked it with his tongue. She touched her tongue to his lips, a movement that seemed to encourage him. His mouth came down on hers with a new intensity while he slowly lifted his hips from hers.

She panicked, not wanting him to leave her. Instinctively she drew her knees up and locked her ankles behind his thighs. He jerked his mouth away from hers and groaned. What had she done? She hadn't wanted to hurt him. She'd only wanted him to— Yes! Like that! She wanted him to stay with her. Oh, and he was. He was... She began to match his rhythm, lifting to meet him, straining to hold him.

He stepped up his pace, moving faster and faster so that she couldn't breathe, couldn't think, could only hold on, tighter and tighter, faster and faster until suddenly... Something seemed to explode inside of her, causing her body to convulse in seismic rippling movements.

Once again Cameron groaned. Then he, too, seemed to lose control, his movements no longer measured as he made one final lunge, burying himself deep within her, holding her as though he never intended to let her go, his face pressed against her neck.

They lay that way for an unmeasurable length of time, his weight pressing her into the bed.

She couldn't remember a time when she had felt so whole and complete. She loved feeling him relaxed in her arms, his breathing harsh in her ear. Lazily she stroked his buttocks and trailed her fingers up to his waist. His skin rippled everywhere she touched, but no other part of him moved.

After a while she lifted her hips tentatively and felt his movement inside. She smiled, then kissed him on his cheek. His hot cheek. His fevered cheek.

Oh, dear Lord. He was sick! How could she have forgotten? How could she have... She struggled to move but it was no use. He was dead weight.

"Cam?" she whispered.

No answer.

Now what? She took a deep breath. He was heavy but not so heavy that she couldn't breathe. She wondered if she could shift him enough to get his medicine. No doubt he was due for more by now. She wriggled until she was able to shift his weight, rolling him onto his back where he stayed without moving.

For a long moment she leaned over him. His pulse had slowed and now had a reassuringly strong rhythm. She felt so limp she could scarcely move. With the last of her energy she filled a glass with water and took one of the tablets out of the bottle.

She raised his head. "Cam? You need to swallow this. Please?" She slipped the tablet between his lips and placed the glass there. He obligingly swallowed the tablet and the water. After she put the glass back on the table she knew she needed to get up, but for the moment all she wanted to do was lie there beside him.

He turned toward her, placing his arm and one of his legs over her, effectively pinning her to his side.

Since there was no place she would rather be, she sighed and closed her eyes. She would stay there just for a few minutes, then she would get up and return to her place on the couch....

Eight

Janine knew she needed to wake up. There were so many things to do. She had to check on Cam to be sure that— Cam! Her eyes snapped open and she found that she was staring into Cameron's eyes from only a few inches away. They were sharing a pillow.

That wasn't all they were sharing, she realized as she discovered she was pressed intimately against him and that he was running his hands over her body, her nude body. Before she could speak, he said, ''Please don't ask me to apologize. I couldn't, not and show any sincerity at all, love. Do you have any idea how long I've wanted to make love to you?''

His words were husky and resonated through her body.

''When I first woke up this morning, I thought I must have dreamed again about making love to you.

Since I've been running this damned fever my dreams have gotten even more erotic. This time I could remember so clearly how you felt when I..." He paused and kissed her. "But then I knew it was much better than anything I had ever dreamed. That's when I realized you were still here in bed with me." He grinned. "I have to admit that you were just what the doctor ordered. I haven't felt this good in a lo-o-ong time."

She could feel herself blushing—all over her body.

"Aw, honey, don't be embarrassed, I was only kidding. Are you upset with me? I don't recall quite how we got started last night. I just remember bits and pieces, but what I do remember was—"

"You were having another nightmare and I tried to wake you up."

"Oh." His expression was uncertain. "Did I force you?"

She had to be honest with him. "Not exactly. You grabbed my wrists and pulled me down and I, uh, I..."

He lifted her wrist and looked at it. "I didn't hurt you, did I? I'm sorry, honey. I wouldn't hurt you for the world."

"You didn't hurt me. I guess the truth is that I've fantasized about you, too. What it would be like if we... Well, anyway, it's over and done with and I—"

He leaned up on his elbow and stared at her with disbelief. "Over and done with? What are you talking about? You make it sound like a smallpox vaccination or something. Is that how you feel? Now that you've experienced your fantasy, it's all over?"

"No, of course not. I just don't exactly know what to say at this point, that's all."

He was quiet for a moment, obviously thinking. When his eyes focused on her once more, he said, "Yes, now I'm beginning to remember more. You were a virgin, weren't you?" When she didn't answer, he repeated, "Weren't you?"

"That doesn't really matter."

"Of course it matters! I was more than half-asleep, still running that damned fever, and I took advantage of you. Otherwise you would never have—"

"No. I could have stopped you. I know I could have. The point is I didn't try because I didn't want to. I enjoyed making love with you. Very much," she admitted.

He smiled. "That's good. So I didn't turn you off the idea."

"Well, no."

He slid his hand over her hips and tugged her close. "That's good," he murmured, dipping his head toward hers and kissing her.

She couldn't think when he kissed her like this. She pulled away and tried to get her breath. "I don't think—" she began.

"Good idea," he murmured, placing a string of kisses along the base of her throat. "It's much better just to feel. This is even better than before. I can see you now and I'm fully awake."

"But, Cam, you've been sick and—"

"And obviously I'm on the mend, wouldn't you say?" He leaned down and pressed his mouth against the tip of her breast. "Mmm," he sighed with obvious pleasure, moving his hand along her thigh.

Her body understood what her mind was attempting to deny. She wanted him even more now that she knew what making love to Cam entailed.

When he raised his head again he looked at her and smiled. "You're shy, aren't you?"

She nodded, unable to find words to explain.

"This is a little more premeditated than last night, isn't it?"

Once again she nodded.

"Will you let me show you what it can be like?" His eyes had lost their teasing glint.

Janine knew that if she said no that he would let her go. Last night had been a spontaneous happening. Now that she had time to think about what they were doing she was afraid. She had never allowed a relationship to go this far, knowing full well that once a man knew the truth about her, he would not consider a serious relationship with her. She hadn't wanted to be hurt, so she had kept herself aloof for years.

This was different. Cam was different. What they shared was very special. Neither of them wanted more than this wonderful friendship. He had made it clear months ago that he never intended to marry again.

Spontaneous or not, they had moved their relationship into intimacy. She had made her choice last night. She wouldn't regret that choice. Not now.

"Show me," she finally whispered, a catch in her voice. Her remaining barriers had come tumbling down.

"What a darling you are," he said, swooping down and giving her a kiss that drove every thought from her mind.

He treated her as though she were a newly discovered treasure to be explored and revered. Each kiss, each caress, elicited a sigh that encouraged him to continue his loving explorations.

Only now she was aware of how sensitive her body was as he caressed her skin with his fingertips and his mouth. Wanting him to experience the same wonderful sensations he was creating within her, she timidly mimicked his movements, eliciting an immediate response that encouraged her to continue with her own explorations.

How wonderfully different a man's body was—the hard muscles covered by satiny smooth skin. She felt so daring, so unlike herself, as she boldly touched him and felt his skin ripple in an instant response.

"I want you so much," he muttered, almost as though he found the admission painful.

She shifted slightly, silently inviting him to take the next step. When he joined them she gave a quick sigh of pleasure, no longer concerned about anything but holding him, following him into new realms of sensuous delight.

She found the slow, very deliberate pace he set increasingly frustrating as her body built up tension. She began to meet his rhythmic movement with thrusts of her own, causing him to falter for a moment before grasping her more tightly and accelerating his movements until she could feel the tension spiraling up and up and—

She cried out when the release hit her, holding him to her as hard as she could, feeling his own body respond to the tremors deep within her. She clutched him to her, reluctant to let go. He rolled onto his side, still holding her against him, and they fell asleep in each other's arms.

Later that morning she was in the kitchen preparing breakfast when he came up behind her and nibbled on the nape of her neck.

"You're supposed to be in bed," she said sternly, although she didn't put much vehemence behind her words.

"But I'm hungry," he complained with a chuckle.

"I'll have your eggs ready for you as soon as the bacon is done."

He slipped his arms around her waist. "That isn't what I'm hungry for." He continued his nibbling.

"Well, that's all you're going to get."

He raised his head. "Really?"

"Really."

"Hmm."

"I'll bring this in to you shortly," she said without looking around.

After a brief silence, he said, "Why can't I eat in here?"

She turned and discovered that he was seated at the table, wearing his freshly laundered jeans and shirt. She sighed, knowing she was going to have some trouble with him. "You're supposed to be resting."

"Can't I rest sitting up?"

She removed the cooked bacon from the skillet, cracked the eggs, and dropped them into the skillet. "I'm sure you can. The question is, will you?"

"Yes. I promise."

He watched as she buttered the toast, placed the eggs on the plate, added the toast and bacon and set the meal in front of him. Then she quickly made a plate for herself and sat down across from him.

"You're a good cook, did you know that?" he asked when they were finished eating.

"Thank you."

"You're awfully quiet."

"Yes."

"You've been thinking."

"Yes."

"Too much."

"Maybe."

"I realized while I was shaving that I didn't use any protection last night or this morning. It's a little late to apologize but I figured that—"

"Don't worry about it."

"Well, actually, I'm not. Because if you should be—"

She put her fork down and looked at him. "You needn't concern yourself. I won't get pregnant."

"You're sure?"

"Yes."

He looked disappointed.

"I forgot to tell you that Trisha wants to see you," Janine said. "She sent that message through Letty when she called yesterday to see how you're doing. If you'd like, I could drive you out to the ranch today. Then if you want to stay—"

"Janine, what's wrong?"

"Nothing's wrong. I just thought—"

"You haven't looked at me since I walked into this kitchen. You haven't looked at me since you got out of bed this morning. I want to know what's wrong."

"What we did was stupid and irresponsible, and I don't wish to discuss it."

He grinned. "Ah. So now you're back to being your prim and proper schoolmarm self."

She took a bite of her toast, chewed several times, then washed it down with a sip of coffee, determined not to allow him to provoke her into saying anything more.

Her silence didn't seem to faze him. In a cheerful voice he said, "You know what I'd really like to do?"

"What?"

"Spend a few days in San Antonio with you. We've spent the past few months doing everything with Trisha. I'd like some time alone with you."

"You've spent the past few days alone with me."

He waved his hand. "That doesn't count. I was out of my head most of the time. I want to spend some time with you when I'm not about to pass out." She tried not to look at him but found it impossible. Slowly her eyes met his. She had seldom seen him so serious. "Please," he said. His eyes were pleading.

Didn't he understand how much she wanted to be with him? She glanced down at her cup. "All right, but only if you promise to get your rest." She knew she was making a mistake, but she couldn't turn down the opportunity to be with him. She loved him.

His smile shattered her with its sweetness. "I promise." He looked at the kitchen clock. "I'll phone

Trisha, and I'll tell Letty where I'll be, while you get ready.''

It took only minutes to clean up the kitchen. Cameron was still on the phone when she went into the bathroom to shower and get dressed. She didn't intend to think of anything more than the moment. Cameron needed to rest and to relax. At least if she stayed with him, he wouldn't go back to work. She knew she was only kidding herself that she was doing it for him, but it helped to know that she was looking after him, as well as collecting memories for herself.

The shrill ringing of his phone shattered the deep night silence, and Cameron groaned, feeling as though he had just fallen asleep. He groped for the lamp switch, turned it on and glanced at the clock. It was almost two o'clock in the morning. Hell, they probably hadn't been asleep more than half an hour.

Janine hadn't moved. He couldn't help but smile, remembering her earlier remark when they had first come to bed and he made it clear that he wasn't the least bit sleepy. In her most prim tone she suggested that the only way he was going to get his needed rest was to stay *out* of bed.

The phone rang again and he grabbed it before the noise awakened her. It was true he had spent a great deal of time these past three days in bed, very few hours of which were spent in sleep. Janine was probably exhausted. He, on the other hand, had never felt better.

"Yes?" he spoke into the receiver.

"Cam? This is Cole."

Cameron sat up. "What's wrong? What's happened?"

Cole gave one of his deep chuckles and said, "Nary a thing, bro. I know I could have waited until morning, but the need to tell you that the twins just arrived into the world safe and sound was too good to keep."

"They're here? But isn't it too soon?"

"Only about three weeks. The doctor was pleased they decided to push up the schedule a little. Clint weighed in at five pounds five ounces, Cade weighed five two. The doctor seemed relieved. He said Allison didn't need them to be any bigger."

"Boys," Cameron breathed. "You weren't sure."

"Nope. The way they were situated in there we couldn't get a clear shot to tell, which is just as well. So now I've got me three boys and a girl. You'd better hurry or you'll never catch up!"

Cameron laughed and glanced around at Janine, who had turned over and was now looking at him with sleep-swollen eyes. "I'm working on it," he said into the phone, grinning.

"Well, what do you know? So Letty was right!" Cole said.

"About what?"

"We're talking about the lady who borrowed Allison's clothes last spring, correct?"

"As much as I hate to admit that Letty's right about anything, in this case, she's right on target."

"So when's the big date?"

"Uh-uh-uh. None of that, now. I've got me a skittish one who's prone to bolt at the least hint of permanence. I've got to handle this one with my customary subtle negotiating and elegant style."

"You mean you haven't asked her?"

"I'm working up to it."

"Well, hell. How much working up do you need?"

"All the time it takes. Tell me where Allison and the babies are, and we'll come see you later on today, after we get some sleep."

"Oh! Sorry. I didn't mean to interrupt anything."

"Just my sleep. I'm trying to get over the flu."

"Yeah, I heard about that. Letty's been keeping us informed about your health."

"She would," he muttered.

Cole told him the name of the hospital in Austin, gave him directions from the interstate, promised him a couple of cigars and hung up.

"I take it Allison had her babies?" Janine asked him when he turned out the light.

He pulled her over until her head was resting on his shoulder. "Yeah. They named them Clint and Cade, another generation of Callaways. Mom and babies are doing fine. I thought we might go see them later today."

When she didn't answer him, he added, "If you want."

"I'd like that," she said softly, after another long pause. "I'd like to thank Allison in person for lending me her clothes last spring."

"And I'd like them to meet you. This will work out just fine." He turned her so that his body was cupped around hers, holding and protecting her. He went to sleep with his hand resting on her breast.

How could she possibly sleep now that she knew she would be meeting more of Cameron's family in a few hours? She lay there, trying to understand what had happened to her during the previous months.

She had been content with her life. She had found a small house that she was seriously considering buying. She enjoyed her job and liked her coworkers. She adored her preschoolers. Before she had met Cameron, she had had everything she wanted in life. Or at least she had everything she had known she could have, given her circumstances.

How had everything changed in such a short while? When she had made her decision to go to the Callaway ranch, she'd had no intention of doing more than speaking with her pupil's father. The last thing she had wanted was to fall in love with him.

And yet...and yet what had occurred between them these past several months had evolved so naturally. They had become friends, sharing their time, their thoughts and eventually their feelings with each other. They had entertained Trisha and, in doing so, had themselves learned how to play again.

And then they had become lovers. How could she possibly regret learning how to fully express her love for this man?

The past few days had been a revelation in so many ways. She had thought she had known Cameron as well as any one person could know another, but she had never seen the playful, very physical, oh so sensual man who had spent hours with her, teaching her so much about herself.

He had teased her about his being the tutor while she was the student, and he had found such interesting ways to praise her for her aptitude and new skills.

Surely they could continue their relationship as it was. Of course they would have Trisha with them, but there would be time for them to have some privacy, as well. He seemed content to spend his spare time with her. Wouldn't that be enough?

When she thought about Cole and Allison and their family, a chill of unease skittered across the surface of her skin. Only time would give her any answers. For now she must rest.

Feeling Cameron's warmth pressed closely to her back helped her to relax. She lifted his hand and placed a kiss in the palm, then allowed it to rest against her breast once more.

What a wonderful way to wake up, she decided with a sleepy smile the next morning as she felt him expertly touching and teasing her. Cameron had learned so much about her these past few days. He had discovered all her pleasure points and explored them with great concentration and intensity whenever given the slightest opportunity. He had obviously found another opportunity.

She opened her eyes, still smiling. "I thought we were going to Austin," she murmured to the man who stared down at her from only a few inches away.

"We are," he responded agreeably, but in no way distracted.

"Then we should probably be getting showered and dressed, don't you think?"

"Excellent idea," he said, but he made no effort to move and since he had very effectively pinned her between him and the bed she could only shake her head and chuckle. "I'll scrub your back," he offered in a helpful tone.

Before she could respond, his mouth found hers and she forgot about everything but Cam—the scent of him, the taste of him, the sound of him, the wonderful sight of him, and most especially the feel of him as he captured her full attention.

She arched into him, taking his fullness, and joined him in a harmony of motion that they had discovered together. She loved this man so much...so very much. How could she possibly give him up, and yet, loving him as she did, how could she possibly hang on to him when she knew the sacrifice he would have to make for them to stay together permanently? She loved him too much to do that to him. She loved him enough to let him go.

But not now, dear God. Please, not now.

They had been on the road for several miles when Cam reached over and took her hand, placing it on his knee. "You've been very quiet this morning. Is something bothering you?"

She smiled. "Not really. I was just thinking about things, that's all."

"What sort of things?"

"Oh... you, your family. I guess I may be a little nervous about meeting them."

"Hey, they're going to love you, I'll guarantee you."

She was quiet for a few more miles before she said, "Tell me something about Cole and Allison. You said they grew up on the ranch together, didn't you?"

"That's right."

"I remember your saying that they have a boy and a girl besides the twins, but I don't recall their ages."

"Tony turned eighteen this summer and is ready for his first year of college. Cole wanted to send him back East to his old alma mater, but Tony wouldn't hear of it. A very independent young man is Tony. He's going to Texas A&M University." He drove for a while before adding, "Katie the terror will be three in September. She was named after Allison's mother, Katherine, and she's a real pistol. Cole adores her."

"That's a considerable gap in ages!"

"Not through Cole's choice, let me tell you. There's quite a story behind that relationship."

"Oh?"

"Not that they would care if you knew about it, of course. You see, a lot of crazy things happened back when our folks were killed. Life for the Callaways was confused and disastrous. Allison and her dad moved away. Cole continued his schooling back East and Cody and I muddled through the best we could with Letty. Four years ago last spring Cole discovered he had a son. Tony."

"Four years ago! You mean all that time he didn't—"

"Yeah. He didn't know that Allison had gotten pregnant. It's all past history now. They managed to get in touch with each other, worked out their problems and got married. Katie arrived stompin', chompin' and rarin' to go a bare nine months after the ceremony, which I thought was downright circumspect of brother Cole, given the circumstances."

"Oh, my!"

"If that wasn't enough, he comes up with twins this time. Guess he wanted to make up for lost time."

"Allison is going to have her hands full," she said faintly, "trying to care for newborn twins and a rowdy three-year-old."

"Oh, Cole's been planning everything. They bought a place on the outskirts of Austin, with plenty of room for growing kids and a studio for Allison. Plus he's hired enough help to keep everything under control and give Allison some time to work."

"I think I'm going to like Allison," she said quietly.

"I have no doubt about that. You're both as independent as hell."

She looked startled. "I don't see myself that way at all. You're always telling me how prim and proper I am."

"Well, I've been chipping away at that prim and proper facade these past few days, and what do I find beneath all that primness? A streak of strong independence."

"Why, Cam, you almost sound insulted."

"It certainly wasn't what I thought I'd have to contend with." He gave her a ferocious scowl.

She reached up and stroked his jaw with her finger in commiseration. He grabbed her hand, pulling her finger to his mouth and nibbling on it. "Mmm-mmm.

You do bring on a powerful hunger in me whenever you're around."

"Cam! Behave!"

"Yes, ma'am." He winked, and she could feel any resistance she might have against this man melt. Independent? Not likely. Not where he was concerned.

She waited at the information desk of the hospital while Cameron parked the car, then they rode the elevator to the maternity floor. They had no more than stepped out of the elevator when Cameron caught her hand and tugged her down the hallway—at almost a sprint—to where a tall slender young man peered into a nursery window.

"So what do you say, Tony?" Cameron asked, clapping him on the shoulder. "Do you think you were ever that small?"

The boy turned around and flashed a smile that was pure Callaway. Although his eyes were dark, his hair was as blond as Cody's. His expressive eyes were glistening with moisture, and Janine realized that he had been touched by the sight of his tiny brothers.

"Hi, Uncle Cam. For your information, I was never that small. Mom said I weighed over eight pounds!" He looked back at the babies. "Aren't they something?"

"Janine, in case you hadn't guessed, this is Tony Alvarez Callaway, my oldest nephew. Tony, this is a friend of mine, Janine Talbot."

The boy ducked his head in a shy nod. "Howdy, ma'am." Then his gaze looked back at the babies. Janine couldn't resist looking, too. The nurses had placed the twins directly in front of the window.

One was on his back, kicking, his face red and his mouth open. The other was on his stomach, his rump in the air, seemingly undisturbed by the ruckus.

"Isn't anybody going to come see what's wrong?" Tony demanded indignantly.

"They aren't going to neglect them, son," a deep voice said from behind them. Janine turned around in time to see Cameron hug the man who had just joined them.

She felt a lump in her throat, seeing the two big men so obviously glad to see each other. Some back pounding ensued, and a couple of cigars were offered and accepted. There was no doubting the love that existed between the three Callaways standing there in the hallway. She looked back at the babies, wondering if they had any idea how lucky they were to be born into such a loving environment.

She was watching one of the nurses pick up the crying baby and take him over to a table where she began to change him when Cameron took her hand and said, "Janine, this is Cole—" he raised their clasped hands "—and Cole, Janine."

"I'm very pleased to meet you, ma'am," Cole drawled, his hand reaching for her other one and squeezing. "I've heard a lot about you. I've been real impatient wondering when I'd get a chance to say hello."

"You've heard about me?" She looked at Cameron uncertainly.

He raised his hand and said, "I swear it wasn't from me, honey. Letty likes to keep everyone current on family business."

Cole tugged her hand slightly and said, "C'mon. I want you to meet Allison." He glowed just saying his wife's name, and once again Janine felt a lump form in her throat. She was aware how little she knew about men, but she was taken aback by these three and their lack of inhibition about showing their feelings. She allowed Cole to lead her down the hallway while Cameron and Tony followed closely behind, talking about school and rodeo events and livestock.

Cole paused just outside the door and tapped, then gently pushed it open. When he saw that Allison was awake, he grinned. "I brought you some company, honey." He released Janine's hand and kept on walking toward the bed where the most beautiful woman Janine had seen in a long while was resting. Her black hair and eyes were a sharp contrast to her fair skin. The look Cole and Allison exchanged was so personal Janine almost blushed.

Cole did the introductions. "This is Janine, honey."

Allison held out her hand and smiled. "At last we meet. Oh, I would have loved to have seen you in my clothes. You must have looked gorgeous in the blues and greens."

Cameron spoke up from somewhere behind Janine. "You got that right. I fell like a downed calf in a roping event, in less than eight seconds flat."

They all laughed, even Janine, although she knew she had turned a fiery hue at his teasing.

Later she didn't remember much about the visit. They didn't stay long, of course, but they were there long enough for her to see that she was learning new meanings for the word family. She was very touched.

She was reminded of her childhood when, before Christmas one year, she had stared at the fairy wonderland in a toy shop's front window, imagining herself small enough to live in the tiny village with all the happy people, singing in the group with a mama, papa and the three children. She would stop each afternoon after school and press her face against the window, absorbed in her dreams.

Once again she was that child, wishing, fantasizing, her face pressed against the glass while she watched the Callaways. But she knew sooner or later she would have to go home and be alone.

Nine

"What did you think of Cole's family?" Cameron asked as they headed south toward San Antonio.

"They're enough to take a person's breath away. I never saw so much energy in one group of people. And you're saying that Katie is just as active."

"At least. Actually, Allison is fairly quiet as a rule, but she's really excited about having the twins here and everything being all right. She wasn't looking forward to those last few weeks of carrying them."

"I can imagine."

They rode along in companionable silence for several miles before Cameron said, "Janine?"

"Mmm?"

"I really appreciate your coming up here with me today."

"I enjoyed it. I really did."

"I've needed this time off. I'm sorry I had to get sick to realize that I've been pushing myself too hard. I don't know what I would have done without you."

"You would have gone to the ranch and Letty would have taken care of you."

"No, I mean it."

She glanced at his frowning profile and said quietly, "So do I. You've got a wonderful family, Cameron. I almost envy what you have, because you aren't even aware of how special it is to have people you can turn to and know that they'll be there for you no matter what."

He reached over and took her hand, placing it on his thigh. "You didn't have that while growing up, did you?"

"No."

"But things are different now, honey. Now you have me."

She tried to tug her hand back, but he wouldn't let her.

"I mean it. You aren't alone anymore."

She gazed at her other hand, lying loosely in her lap. "I know."

"There's so much I want to say to you, but dammit, I'm afraid."

She looked at him in surprise. "You? Cameron, you're not afraid of anything."

"I am where you're concerned. I'm afraid of losing you."

"I'm right here."

"You know what I mean."

"No, I don't. We're friends, Cam. That's very precious to me, something I've never had before, a friendship with a man. You've made it very special for me."

"But I want so much more!" he burst out.

She tugged her hand away and clasped her hands together in her lap. "Yes, I know."

"Seeing them today made me remember how happy I was when Trisha was born."

"Were you sorry she was a girl?"

"Of course not! I wanted whatever the baby turned out to be, but I wanted more. Andrea and I had planned to have several children and..." He shook his head in irritation. "But things happened and..."

"Yes, things happen, and life doesn't always work out the way we plan."

"I never dreamed I could love anyone else, and yet when I met you I felt like a schoolboy all over again, with a gigantic crush."

She smiled at his description and his wry tone of voice. "You certainly didn't act like a schoolboy. Those were some very experienced moves you were putting on me, mister."

"Don't you see, honey? We're so good together. You've made me laugh again and love again and want again. The world is mine again. I want it all—and I want it with you."

She didn't say anything. She couldn't, not after such a declaration. She knew exactly how he felt, because she felt the same way. The only difference was that she knew the world wasn't hers. She knew she couldn't have it all.

He deserved to have everything he wanted.

"How are you feeling?" she said, and he looked at her as though she had just lost her mind. What kind of question was that to ask at a time like this? she knew he must be thinking.

"I'm fine. Why?"

"Are you tired?"

"Not particularly."

"Are you up to driving me home? I've been away for several days and I need to get back."

"I don't want to, no. But if you feel you need to go home, of course I'll take you."

"Thank you," she whispered, her throat clogging with emotion.

They stopped in San Antonio long enough for her to pack the few things she had brought with her, then continued south, saying very little.

When they drove up in front of her house, she turned to him and said, "You're welcome to stay here, if you'd like."

He shook his head. "No. I want to check on Trisha. It's time I talked to her about moving to San Antonio. I've been putting it off, hoping that I could tell her that..." He shook his head. "Hell, I don't know. I guess I've been fantasizing too much lately, hoping things would change. Hoping that..." He ran his hand through his hair in disgust.

"Let me be your friend, Cam. Please? It's very important that I don't lose you from my life."

His head jerked up and he looked at her with new alertness. "It is?"

"Of course."

"I thought that you were letting me know I was taking up too much of your time."

"On the contrary. I'm taking up too much of yours. It's obvious that you want a wife and family. I can't give you that. You need to find someone who can."

"Just because you never had a family doesn't mean you can't learn to become a part of one. Why, you, Trisha and I are already a family, if you could only understand. It isn't something you have to learn to do. It's just something you become. It's part of being."

She leaned over and kissed him, then slowly pulled away. "Give Trisha my love. I'm sorry she won't be attending our school in the fall, but I think you're doing the best thing for both of you." She slipped out of the car and picked up her bag. "Take care now. Don't work so hard. Maybe we can get together some weekend once you have Trisha settled in."

She turned away, proud of herself for sounding so light, pleased that she hadn't broken down. She unlocked the front door and stepped inside the empty little house, then closed the door and waited for the sound of his car to drive away. Only then did she allow herself to give vent to the grief and pain she had locked away these past few hours. Dry sobs began to tear from her tight throat while she slowly sank to the floor, her back against the door, sobbing for something she could never have, no matter how much she wanted it.

"Daddy, Daddy, did you know that Auntie Allison had her twin babies and their names are Clint and Cade and they're little bitty, only about this big—"

she demonstrated with her hands "—and Auntie Allison said that when they get some bigger she'll bring them to see me and let me hold them. And when they get big I can help 'em walk and—"

"Whoa, hold it! Hold it! Don't plot out their whole lives right at the moment, sugar. Let's let them be little babies for a while, okay?"

"Okay." She hugged him tightly around the knees. "I love you, Daddy. I wish we could have twins, then I could have someone to play with all the time and I wouldn't have to wait so long for 'em to come see me."

Picking her up, Cameron went down the hallway, looking for his aunt. "Well, it would be a little difficult for you and me to have twins on our own, punkin," he said absently. "Letty?" he called.

"She's resting in her room," Trisha said obligingly. "Maybe Missy Talbot would like to have some twins for us. Could we ask her, Daddy?"

Cameron felt a pang shoot through him in the region of his heart. "I don't think so, baby. Ms. Talbot already has a full-time job."

"But lots of mommies work. And 'member that lady who bringed us our food that one time and she called me Missy Talbot's little girl?"

"Yes, darling. I remember quite well. Ms. Talbot was embarrassed by the waitress's mistake, wasn't she? Her cheeks got all pink."

Trisha giggled. "But she liked it, too. I could tell. Couldn't you?"

"I thought so at the time," he murmured. Attempting to change the subject, he asked, "Has your uncle Cody been here since the twins were born?"

"Uh-uh. Aunt Letty said she didn't know what she was gonna do 'bout him, 'cause she never knew where to find him when she needed him."

"Yeah, well. He'll show up one of these days. I know he'll be glad to know everyone's all right."

He walked into the family room and sank onto the couch with Trisha on his knee. "So tell me what you've been up to, young lady," he said, knowing that if he could just concentrate on his daughter, he could lessen the pain around his heart.

Three days had gone by since Cameron had dropped Janine off at her house. Three days since she had heard from him. It seemed like three years.

She had grown accustomed to being with him day and night since his illness. She'd had a heck of a time trying to fall asleep last night. Why hadn't anyone told her that once she had gotten used to sleeping with someone else she would have difficulty sleeping alone?

There was so much she didn't know.

Now she industriously worked in her yard each morning before the temperature soared. She found it soothing to be a part of the earth, as though it connected her somehow with the world. She was having trouble trying to reestablish her old routine, the one she had had before Cameron had become such a major force in her life.

She had always managed to keep herself busy, so why did there seem to be so much extra time in her day now? She would be glad when school started again.

She paused, listening. Was that the phone? With the house shut up because of the air-conditioning, she didn't ordinarily hear the phone. She scrambled to her feet and dashed to the house. As she tore open the back screen door, then the wooden one, she heard the phone ring once again. She raced to grab it.

"Hello?.. hello?"

There was nothing but a dial tone.

Nothing in this world was more frustrating than a ringing phone that stopped ringing just before a person answered it! She slammed down the phone.

Whoever it was would call back if it was important. It probably wasn't important. It was probably one of her friends calling about lunch, or possibly a movie, or maybe...

Who was she kidding? She wanted it to be Cameron. She didn't know where he was. He might have gone back to San Antonio. He might be at work. He might have gone back to Austin, or even Dallas, or Fort Worth, or Houston. He might be anywhere.

Or he might still be at the ranch, only a half hour's drive away.

The only way to find out was to call.

Did she have the courage? After all, they were friends, weren't they? So what was wrong with a friend calling another friend? Just because he was a male didn't make him off-limits. They were used to talking to each other every day. It had been three days.

She would consider calling him.

But first, she would finish her yard work. Then she would take a shower, get cleaned up a little, put on some makeup...

To make a phone call?

Okay, so maybe she was going a little overboard. She needed to lighten up a little, see the humor in the situation. There was no reason to see it as a major tragedy. Just because she wasn't going to marry him didn't mean they couldn't continue their relationship—their wonderfully intimate, excitingly erotic relationship.

Besides, he had never *asked* her to marry him, so it wasn't as though she had turned him down or anything. He certainly wasn't an unrequited lover.

Who was she kidding? Why should he ask when she had already made her feelings on the subject abundantly clear? Unless a person was really into feeling the pangs of rejection, he wouldn't see a need to pose the question, would he?

Well?

So maybe he was feeling a little rejected at the moment. Who could blame him? Maybe he would like to hear from her. Maybe she would invite him and Trisha to dinner, if he was still at the ranch. Why not?

By the time she reached this decision, she had finished the yard, taken her shower, put on a clean pair of shorts and matching top, arranged her hair and was finishing applying the last touches of makeup.

She smiled at her reflection. That was the most cheerful she had looked in three days.

She marched to the phone and dialed the ranch's number. It was answered on the third ring.

"Hello," she said in her most professional voice. "This is Janine Talbot, and I was wondering if you could tell me where I might find Cameron Callaway."

"Oh, hi, Ms. Talbot, this is Rosie. I don't know where he is at the moment, exactly. Everyone's been outside most of the morning trying to find Trisha. He came in for a little while, but he's gone out again."

"Trisha? Trying to find her? She's lost?"

"We're not sure. Either lost or hiding somewhere. It's anybody's guess. Cameron said they'd had words this morning, and she'd run out of the room crying. He said he decided to give them both some time before he went looking for her. When he did, he couldn't find her anywhere."

"You've looked through the house?"

"Oh, yes, ma'am. About six of us looked everywhere we could think a five-year-old might hide. At first, Cameron was angry, but now I think he's more scared than anything. If she left the surrounding ranch buildings, she'll be next to impossible to find."

"Oh, no! This is awful. Should I come out?"

"I'm sure Cameron would like to know you're concerned, but you do whatever you think is best."

"I'll be right here," she said. Within minutes, she was in the car and pulling out of her driveway.

At the Big House she hurried to the door and knocked. Cameron was the one who answered it. When he saw her, he grabbed her and held on as though afraid to let go.

"This is all my fault. I was in a bad mood and I took it out on her. I was so stupid. I wasn't thinking about how she would react and I just—"

"It's okay, love," she murmured, holding him tightly. "She's okay. I'm sure of it. She's a smart little girl. She wouldn't put herself in any danger."

"But we've looked everywhere around here. And we've called and called. Alejandro has been rounding up his men. They're going to start riding out, looking for her."

"Surely she wouldn't have left the immediate area."

He shook his head, still buried in her hair. "Who knows? My biggest fear is that somehow one of our family enemies has found her. Up until now we've only received property damage, nothing that threatened a person's life, but then I think about the wrecks. If they were intentional, then we have a deadly killer somewhere out there, waiting. What if they came to the ranch? What if they saw her? I've been going out of my mind thinking about all the possibilities."

They stood there in silence for the longest while. Janine knew he was drawing strength from her being there. Thank heaven she had decided to call him.

"Ah, you're here!" Letty said behind them. "Good thing. This man's about driven us all crazy for the past three days. I hope this means that whatever you two quarreled about has been made up, because I never want to be around him in this mood again!"

Janine took Cameron's hand and opened the door. "C'mon. We can talk later. Right now we're going to find a missing five-year-old."

In the end, it was Janine who found her—for the simple reason that she didn't go into the hunt with any preconceived notions. Everyone else knew that there were definite areas where Trisha was forbidden to go. They knew it; she knew it. And Trisha had never defied those orders before.

Somehow Janine knew that today was different. Something had happened between father and daughter that had caused a rift between them, something that had never happened before.

She also knew Trisha, after having spent the past several months in her company. She was a very self-possessed, strong-willed and, yes, stubborn young lady.

So Janine stood in the ranch yard and looked all around her, studying the scene. If she were a five-year-old in a tantrum, where would she be most likely to go? After standing there absorbing her surroundings for several minutes, she started toward the barn.

"She wouldn't be in the barn. She knows better," Cameron said, following her. "It's too dangerous. We keep the horses in there, plus a bunch of our equipment. There's hay and—" Janine wasn't stopping, so he added, "Besides, we looked in there.'

"Yes, but you really didn't expect to find her, did you?"

"Not really, no. Like I just said—"

"It's amazing how you can overlook something when you don't expect to see it there."

She paused just inside the large doorway, letting her eyes adjust to the dimness of the inside. She heard a sound to the left of the doorway and looked over. One of the barn cats wandered out to see if the stranger was there to feed her. Although skinny, the cat was obviously nursing.

Kittens. Uh-huh. And where would a cat hide her kittens?

She walked over to the storage area where the cat had come from and looked around. There were no hiding places for a litter of kittens. Then she saw the ladder going up into the loft above. She immediately crossed to it and started climbing.

"My God! She wouldn't have tried something like that! Why, she could break her neck!" Cameron exclaimed. But Janine ignored him. She was following her instincts. She couldn't explain to him what she was thinking and feeling. She just had to go with it.

As soon as she reached the top, she crawled onto the hay and looked around. The loft was enormous. They could be anywhere.

She didn't bother to call Trisha's name. If the girl was here she would have heard them calling earlier; she had refused to answer then, so she wouldn't answer now. Janine stood, dusting her hands and knees, and began to explore.

By the time she found the corner where the three tiny kittens were curled up asleep, Cameron had joined the hunt, working the opposite side of the loft.

"Over here, Cam," she said softly. He immediately turned and hurried to where she stood.

Trisha had fallen asleep not far from the kittens. Her face was smudged with dust and tears, her blouse torn, and her hair was filled with bits of hay. Still, she looked quite unharmed.

Cameron knelt beside her. "Trisha?" he said, touching her lightly on her cheek. She stirred sluggishly. Her eyes looked puffy from crying. When she finally opened them, they seemed almost too heavy to keep open and they fell back shut.

"Trisha, honey, what are you doing up here?"

The child shifted and stretched out her legs. She again opened her eyes, this time focusing on her father. "Daddy?"

"Yes, darling. I'm right here."

Janine could hear the huskiness in his voice and experienced a similar choking sensation.

"Daddy? Did you know we have kittens? I saw the mama cat and she ran up the ladder like a fireman and I followed her to see where she went. Then she feeded her babies and she let me watch and then . . . and then . . ." She shrugged. "I guess I fell asleep."

"I guess you did. Didn't you hear me calling you?"

She shook her head.

"Are you sure?"

She looked surprised that he asked. "Uh-huh." Obviously it had never occurred to her to lie about anything.

"Well, it's past lunchtime and you've had everybody worried out of their minds. I think we should go tell them you're okay, don't you?"

She nodded solemnly and came to her feet. Only when she turned to go to the ladder did she see Janine, who had retreated to the exit of the loft when Cameron first started speaking to his daughter.

"Missy Talbot! You came to see us. Daddy said you prob'ly wouldn't come but you did!" She staggered through the hay and hugged Janine.

"Yes. I was sorry you weren't at the house when I got here," she said, stroking the little girl's curls.

"Yeah," Trisha agreed.

Cameron joined them and one by one they climbed down the ladder, Cameron going first, followed by Trisha, so that he could make sure she didn't slip.

Janine stayed quiet as Cameron sent out word that Trisha had been found. Then he took his daughter into the house and upstairs to clean her up and, as he put it, to give her the talking to of her life for scaring them all to death.

Letty suggested she and Janine go ahead with lunch, since she had a hunch he would be a while.

While they ate, Letty asked questions about the twins and if she had had a chance to meet Katie and what she had thought about the visit. Janine realized later that she had been so caught up in answering all the questions that she didn't have an opportunity to get nervous about talking to Cameron.

When Cameron came down later he waved off the idea of food and just had some iced tea.

"I had to set some strict punishment for this one. I told her she couldn't come downstairs for the rest of the day. She was crushed. She's been wanting to see you," he said to Janine. "She also solemnly promised me that she will not go anywhere on the ranch that has been set off-limits again."

"And you believed her," Janine said with a grin.

He looked surprised. "Of course!"

Janine laughed. "Ah, the joys of parenthood. Hope springs eternal, and all that stuff."

"Do you think she lied?"

"Of course not. I think she is an inquisitive little girl. She will remember for a while. Then, as she gets

older, and more and more alluring things are just beyond the rules . . ."

"I guess you know kids pretty well," he said glumly.

"She should," Letty said, pushing back her chair.
"She's looked after enough of 'em. Now, if you two
will excuse me, I've had about as much excitement as
my ole bones can handle for one day. I'm goin' upstairs to rest for a while. I'll see you two later." She
paused and peered over her glasses. "You *are* staying
for dinner now, aren't you, Ms. Talbot? I'm not sure
I'll want to be around Cameron tonight if you don't."

Janine grinned. "Thank you, Letty. I'd like to
stay."

"Then I'll come back down later," she said tartly.
"Otherwise I might have had 'em send me something
to eat in my room." She left without a backward
glance.

Cameron looked at Janine and said, "Let's go into
the other room. We need to talk."

He led the way into the study. When she walked
through the doorway, he closed and locked the door.
"So we won't be disturbed," he said, waving her to
have a seat. The room was lined with bookshelves.
There was a large desk and chair at one end of the
room, a comfortable-looking sofa and a grouping of
chairs at the other. She sank onto the sofa and looked
at him.

He sat at the other end, facing her.

"I don't understand. I just don't."

She could see he was hurting. The pain had etched
lines in his face that hadn't been there just a few days

earlier. She owed him an explanation, no matter how painful it was for her to talk about.

"You are a natural at mothering, Janine. You understand children so well. It's an innate gift, an extra sense that seems to tune you into them. And yet you keep insisting you don't want to marry and have a family. Is it just me? I mean, are you looking for someone who could be a perfect parent so that—"

"No, it's not that at all, Cam." She moved closer so that she could touch him. "Please. It isn't you at all. It's me. Don't you see? I'm the one who's defective."

"Defective! What the hell are you talking about? There's not a damned thing wrong with you!"

She took his hand and held it up to her cheek, rubbing her head against his hand much like a cat wanting to be stroked.

When she began to talk, her words were choppy. "I've never talked about this. Not with anyone. I never intended to say anything. Not ever. But you deserve to know, Cam. I love you too much not to tell you."

"You love me?" His eyes suddenly seemed to fill with light.

"Oh, yes. How could you possibly doubt it?"

"Well, for a while I thought it was possible. But then...when you said...and I thought..." He shrugged helplessly.

"Make no mistake about it, Cameron Callaway. I love you absolutely."

"Then for God's sake marry me! Put me out of my misery!"

"Marrying me would only add to your misery. I love you too much to subject you to a future with me. Please try to understand."

He shook his head. "I'm trying, believe me. But you aren't making any sense."

"When I was sixteen, I was in an automobile accident with the boy I was dating at the time. It was a wonder we both weren't killed. The other driver was, and there was some doubt that I would recover."

"You! But you're in perfect health. You're—"

"Most of the injuries were internal. You may have thought I was overly modest when we've been together, but I'm still self-conscious about the scars on my abdomen."

"I've never noticed them."

She smiled. "Good."

"So you are saying that because of your scars you don't want to marry me? They don't matter. You should know me better than that."

"Cameron, my internal injuries were very extensive. I was hemorrhaging severely. The doctors on duty did whatever they could to save my life. If they had had more time perhaps they might have attempted to repair some of the damage. But they were more concerned with stopping the bleeding."

"I had no idea you'd gone through so much. Thank God you managed to live through it."

"Yes. I'm very thankful. But when they first told me what they had done, I wished at first that I *had* died."

"Janine!"

"I know. That's very selfish of me, particularly when you lost your wife and I was so filled with self-pity that I could wish away my life." This was much, much harder to tell than she had imagined. She had hoped that he would have guessed, but he showed no sign of understanding. "I can't have children, Cameron. That's what I've been trying to tell you. They had to remove everything. I was given no choice. It was done before I even regained consciousness. At the time they weren't sure that I would regain consciousness. It's a fact I've had to live with ever since."

His face drained of all color. She knew what a shock her news must be to him. But now that she had finally told him, she felt better. She had finally, at long last, shared the knowledge with another person. Somehow in the sharing, she had halved her pain. Unfortunately she had given it to him, something she had hoped never to have to do.

"Oh, God, love. I had no idea. Not even when you spoke of the surgery. I don't know what awful secret I thought you were trying to share with me. I just didn't consider it was that."

"I know."

"You love children so much."

"Yes. Yes, I do. That's why I decided to work with them. It's been a wonderful way to have children in my life."

He pulled her into his arms and held her close.

She knew that now he had received the shock of her news, he would recover more quickly and get on with his life. She hoped they would continue to be friends and knew that one day he would meet someone who would make the perfect mother for the children he wanted to have.

At the moment, though, she couldn't face the thought of seeing him with another woman. Perhaps that would change in time. Perhaps her love for him could continue to grow enough to encompass even that possibility.

He pulled away and she saw the tears in his eyes. "I was such a fool, carrying on about wanting a larger family. No wonder you— I'm sorry, love. So sorry."

"Please don't be. How could you know? I just thought you needed to understand why I'll never marry anyone."

He grew still and stared at her so intently that she began to feel uncomfortable. "What did you just say?"

"That you needed to—"

"No. That last part."

"You mean that I'll never marry?"

"Yes. Would you kindly explain how your not being able to have children has anything at all to do with your getting married?"

Now she was having trouble understanding him. What sort of silly question was that?

"Well, really, Cam, I think the answer is obvious, don't you?"

"No. Suppose you explain it to me."

She shrugged, trying to hide her irritation. "Every man who marries expects to have a family—it goes without saying."

"Does it?"

"When Bobby found out what had happened to me, he was terribly sorry. He even blamed himself for the accident, which was silly. He probably saved my life. He explained that everything had changed for us after the accident. He was very uncomfortable. So was I. He didn't have to tell me how he felt. We had talked about getting married some day. We'd even picked out names for our children...."

Cameron muttered an unprintable word, which caused her to jump. "So on the basis of one person's reaction, you decided that absolutely no man would want to marry you if you couldn't have children."

She clasped her hands and looked down at them in her lap. "My father left when my mother couldn't have more children."

"God help us," he muttered. She wasn't certain if he was praying or cursing.

"Janine, would you look at me? Please?"

She glanced up and was relieved to see that his face had color once again.

"I am sorrier than I can say that the men in your life felt the need to father children so strongly that they would base major decisions on such an issue. However, I do not happen to share that particular philosophy. Besides, I've already fathered a child, a beautiful little girl who gives me a great deal of pleasure—except when she falls asleep in a hayloft and scares the living daylights out of me." He shifted, his arm going around her while he tilted her face up to his.

"Now listen to me very, very carefully. I am only going to say this once, and then I never want to discuss the subject again. Do you hear me?"

She nodded. How could she not hear him? He was only a few inches away from her.

"I love you, Janine Talbot. You brought me back to life again. I had buried myself away from everything that was good and happy and funny and alive. Then one rainy morning you came marching into my life and gave me hell, turning my life upside down and sideways. It's never been the same since. And that's just fine with me."

He stroked a wisp of hair from her cheek. "Now then. Words can't begin to describe the devastation I feel where you are concerned, to know that you have suffered so many years thinking that no one would want to marry you because of your situation. You are wrong, Janine Talbot. Very, very wrong."

She heard the words all right, but their meaning was slow to sink in. When it did, Janine felt a flush envelop her and her heart started pounding in her chest.

"Not only do I love you to distraction," he went on, "but I fully intend to marry you. I will not take no for an answer, do you hear me?

"Yes, it's a shock to discover that you aren't going to be able to have my children. I've spent months fantasizing about how to act if I *accidentally* got you pregnant. I guess I hoped that if you did get pregnant, I wouldn't have to figure out a subtle way to let you know how desperately I wanted to marry you.

"The fact is, I'm shy as hell when it comes to saying things like 'I love you' and 'I want to marry you.'" He paused for a moment, then grinned. "Actually, that didn't hurt at all. Maybe I'll get more comfortable with practice. The thing is, we are already a family, don't you know that? You, me and Trisha have become a family. You just must have missed it, or maybe it's because you didn't know what a real family was. Well, I'm telling you. You're already a part of one. You're a Callaway in everything but the name, and I intend to fix that as soon as I can."

He stroked her cheek with his thumb, wiping away the tears streaming from her eyes. "Oh, baby, I wish I'd known. We could have saved ourselves so much grief if only you'd told me sooner."

"But, Cam," she said, brokenly, "you wanted more children." She gave a slight hiccup, then buried her head in his shoulder.

"There are so many children who need a home, honey. You know that. We can have as many children as we want. We can plan for them. We can adopt an infant, or an older child. There's so much we can do. There's so much love to share. Let's don't waste any of it, okay?"

When she didn't answer, he leaned back and looked at her face. "Why are you still crying?"

"B-because I—I'm s-so-o-o-o haappy."

"Good. Then I'll take that to mean yes, you'll marry me. Is that right?"

She nodded vigorously into his shoulder.

"Immediately?"

She pulled away. "Immediately?" she squeaked, wiping at her eyes.

"Well, yes. You see—" he actually looked sheepish "—I, uh, thought that, to convince Trisha she should move to San Antonio and live with me full-time, I could tell her you would be there, too. Remember I tried to get you to come last spring as a housekeeper-nanny, and you said no? So I have hired a house-keeper—who will look after Trisha when you have to be at school—so maybe you'll come as my wife and Trisha's mother. Would you consider that?''

''Oh Cam,'' she said in a wavering voice.

''Please don't start crying again, okay? Anyway, since school starts in a couple of weeks, I thought if we got married right away, that would give us some time for a honeymoon. Not that I haven't enjoyed our recent rehearsals or any—ouch—thing, but, oh, Janine, honey, I love you so much.''

She no longer felt like waiting for him to kiss her, so she kissed him. She put all the expertise she had learned from him into it, taking her time and making certain that he understood just how much she *had* learned.

She also began to unsnap his shirt, running her hands across his chest and down to his belt buckle. She felt him suck in his breath, inadvertently leaving enough room for her fingers to slide beneath the belt and touch him. ''I'm ready whenever you are, dar-lin','' he whispered, nipping her ear. ''You'll never have to doubt that.''

With a sudden sense of reckless freedom, Janine reached down and unfastened her shorts. ''Let the honeymoon begin,'' she said with a chuckle.

''Yes, ma'am!''

*   *   *   *   *

Take 4 bestselling love stories FREE

Plus get a FREE surprise gift!

In the spirit of Christmas, Silhouette invites
you to share the joy of the holiday season.

Experience the beauty of Yuletide romance with Silhouette
Christmas Stories 1992—a collection of heartwarming stories by
favorite Silhouette authors.

JONI'S MAGIC by Mary Lynn Baxter
HEARTS OF HOPE by Sondra Stanford
THE NIGHT SANTA CLAUS RETURNED by Marie Ferrarella
BASKET OF LOVE by Jeanne Stephens

This Christmas you can also receive a FREE keepsake Christmas
ornament. Look for details in all November and December
Silhouette books.

Also available this year are three popular early editions of
Silhouette Christmas Stories—1986, 1987 and 1988. Look for these
and you'll be well on your way to a complete collection of the
best in holiday romance.

Share in the celebration—with Silhouette's
Christmas gift of love.

SX92

It's Opening Night in October—
and you're invited!
Take a look at romance with a
brand-new twist, as the stars
of tomorrow make their
debut today!
It's LOVE:
an age-old story—
now, with
*WORLD PREMIERE
APPEARANCES* by:

Patricia Thayer—Silhouette Romance #895
JUST MAGGIE—Meet the Texas rancher who wins this pretty
teacher's heart...and lose your own heart, too!

Anne Marie Winston—Silhouette Desire #742
BEST KEPT SECRETS—Join old lovers reunited and see what
secret wonders have been hiding...beneath the flames!

Sierra Rydell—Silhouette Special Edition #772
ON MIDDLE GROUND—Drift toward Twilight, Alaska, with this
widowed mother and collide—heart first—into body heat
enough to melt the frozen tundra!

Kate Carlton—Silhouette Intimate Moments #454
KIDNAPPED!—Dare to look on as a timid wallflower blos-
soms and falls in fearless love—with her gruff, mysterious
kidnapper!

**Don't miss the classics of tomorrow—
premiering today—only from**

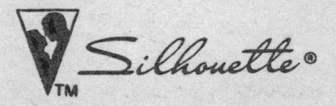

PREM

TAKE A WALK ON THE DARK SIDE OF LOVE

October is the shivery season, when chill winds blow and shadows walk the night. Come along with us into a haunting world where love and danger go hand in hand, where passions will thrill you and dangers will chill you. Come with us to

In this newest short story collection from Sihouette Books, three of your favorite authors tell tales just perfect for a spooky autumn night. Let Anne Stuart introduce you to "The Monster in the Closet," Helen R. Myers bewitch you with "Seawitch," and Heather Graham Pozzessere entice you with "Wilde Imaginings."

Silhouette Shadows™
Haunting a store near you this October.

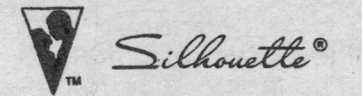